WHITE WIG

A passenger is found shot dead in his seat on a London bus when it reaches its terminus. Apart from the driver and conductor, there have only been two other passengers on the bus, a white-haired man and a masculine-looking woman, who both alighted separately at earlier stops. To the investigating police, the conductor is the obvious suspect, and he is held and charged. The man's fiancée hires private detective Paul Rivington to prove his innocence — and it turns out to be his most extraordinary and dangerous case to date . . .

GERALD VERNER

WHITE WIG

Complete and Unabridged

LINFORD
Leicester

First published in Great Britain

First Linford Edition
published 2017

A catalogue record for this book is available
from the British Library.

ISBN 978–1–4448–3241–9

Published by
F. A. Thorpe (Publishing)
Anstey, Leicestershire

Set by Words & Graphics Ltd.
Anstey, Leicestershire
Printed and bound in Great Britain by
T. J. International Ltd., Padstow, Cornwall

This book is printed on acid-free paper

1

The Last Passenger

In spite of the rain and hail and the wild soughing of the wind, the bus steadily breasted the hill that runs from Southend Pond to the London Road and leads eventually into Bromley North. Harry Mace, the driver, had great difficulty in keeping the machine from skidding, and was feeling heartily glad that he had nearly reached the end of the journey and the day's work. Every now and again he had to shake his head to clear his eyes from the hail that the wind dashed into his face over the screen. At times the force was so strong that the little pieces of frozen rain cut into the skin, making it smart and burn.

He was glad that his friend, Dick Lonsdale, was less exposed on the conductor's platform, for Dick had had a bad time in the upheaval that people called the Great War, and had been far from well during the past two days.

The bus was a 'pirate', plying for hire between Charing Cross and Bromley Common, and owned jointly by Mace and Lonsdale. The two men had fought together in Flanders, and a friendship that had started in a welter of blood and mud had continued after demobilisation and eventually led to the purchase of the Blue Moon. They had called it this in memory of a certain little café near Ypres, where they had met for the first time.

Through Bromley North with its quaint old Market Place, now almost obliterated by the driving rain, the motor-bus crawled; down the incline, past Bromley South Station, round the bend, and up the slope of Mason's Hill. It had reached the top of the rise when Dick decided to brave the storm of hail and rain and reverse the boards on the front, in readiness for the morning journey. It was an open-topped, old-fashioned bus, and it was a habit of his to do so at this stage of the route, and in spite of the weather he almost mechanically went through his usual procedure.

He ran up the steps, and as he reached

the top an unusually heavy gust of wind made him stagger and grip the rail. As he recovered his balance he saw the solitary outside passenger rise and move towards him. Guessing that he was about to alight, Dick rang the bell and stood on one side for the old man to pass. He wished him good night as he groped his way down the steps, but the old man made no reply. Perhaps he was a little deaf, thought Dick, and after waiting to give him sufficient time to get off, he gave a double ring for Mace to proceed.

The bus started with a slight jerk that almost caused Dick to lose his balance. He retained his feet, however, by clutching at the nearest seat, and as the bus got going he began to walk unsteadily towards the front. Without any particular reason, his thoughts turned to the solitary passenger who had just left. Dick put him down as being a trifle eccentric, for there was no reason why he should have continued to occupy an outside seat on such a night.

He had boarded the bus at Charing Cross, just as it was on the point of departure. It had been fairly full then, and Dick had felt rather reluctant to send the old man upstairs. At Lewisham Obelisk, however, several people had got off, and he had taken the trouble to go up and tell the old man that there was room inside. All he had received in reply was a grunt. Seeing that the solitary passenger apparently preferred the discomforts of the wet exterior to the comparative dryness of the interior, Dick had left him alone and gone back to his platform.

From this passenger in particular, his thoughts turned to the peculiarities of passengers in general as he leaned over the front of the swaying bus and tugged at the indicator boards. They fitted into two iron slots, and, probably owing to the wood having swollen with the wet had stuck, and in spite of his most strenuous efforts he was unable to shift them. He banged and thumped and pulled without result. The boards refused to move.

At that moment the bus reached Homesdale Road, and at a jerk of the bell from a passenger below it came to a standstill. Dick Lonsdale was rather glad of the respite, for the movement of the bus and the buffeting of the wind were both factors

4

that had contributed to his unsuccessful attempts to move the boards. Now getting a grip with both hands, he managed, after a series of jerks and thumps, to free them. By the time he had done this, the bus had been standing nearly a minute, and he hastily stamped twice for Mace to proceed. It was useless trying to re-insert the boards until they had dried, so he laid them under one of the seats and made his way downstairs, glad to be under shelter once more. Glancing inside the bus, he saw that only one passenger remained, and he was apparently dozing, for his head had dropped forward on his chest as though the storm had acted as a soporific and lulled him to sleep.

The woman who had been the only other inside passenger must have got off at Homesdale Road. She had been rather a queer customer. In spite of her dress, she had looked more like a man than a woman, and a rather sinister-looking man at that. Tall, gaunt, and angular, with a weather-beaten face and iron grey hair, little wisps of which had blown free from her confining hat, she had boarded the bus at the Obelisk and plumped herself down in the seat next to the door. Owing to her enormous height, her feet had reached to the centre of the gangway, and to Dick's astonishment had been encased in a pair of men's hobnailed boots. They had been so huge and ungainly that they held his attention with an almost eerie fascination The woman had a bag full of provisions by her side, and in her hand a heavy stick that ended in a clumsy knob. Dick had put her down as one of the many gipsies in the district.

It was one of Dick's hobbies to study the various passengers who travelled on the Blue Moon, and very interesting he found it. It helped to break the monotony of collecting fares, and passed the time. He was still ruminating about the extraordinary-looking woman when they reached the Dairy Farm, and he had to force his mind away from that strange individual and attend to the usual odd jobs that had to be done before leaving the bus for the night.

Harry Mace gave a sigh of relief as he pulled up in front of the Barley Mow. It has been a tiring run, but now there only remained a quarter of a mile's drive to

Merrion's Riding School, where the bus was garaged, and then the short walk with Dick to his mother's house, where there would be the certainty of hot coffee and a square meal.

The wind was still for a moment, and Mace heard his friend's call: 'All change, please!' He waited for the usual signal to run the empty bus up the road to the garage, but the signal never came. Instead he heard a smothered cry from inside the bus and the sound of stumbling footsteps coming round the side. Looking down from the height of his driving seat, he gazed into the white, upturned face of his friend.

'What's the matter?' he asked anxiously as he swung himself out of the seat under the mackintosh cover and descended into the streaming roadway. 'Feeling queer?'

Dick shook his head, and without speaking beckoned Mace towards the back of the bus. With his hand on the rail and his foot on the step, he seemed to regain both his composure and his speech.

'Come inside,' he said a trifle huskily. 'Something odd has happened.' He led the way up the gangway, followed by Mace, and

7

stopped within a few feet of the front seat.

The solitary passenger still sat there, one arm hanging limply down by his side. He was a man of about seventy, and the cut of his clothes and the large horn-rimmed glasses he wore suggested that he was an American. Very still he sat, with his head drooping on his breast.

'Let me look at him,' broke in Harry, pushing his friend aside. 'It may be a heart attack.' He stooped over the motionless figure on the seat and opened the coat. 'Good God!' His voice rose to an unnatural shrillness as he turned a frightened face to Dick. 'He's been shot!'

2

A Client for Mr. Rivington

Mr. Paul Rivington laid down his pen, blotted the page he had just written, and read it through. The big desk was littered with sheets of manuscript, and when he had digested the contents of the one he held in his hand he collected the others together and fastened them with a paper clip.

'That's another chapter done, Bob,' he remarked, rising with a sigh of relief and lighting a cigarette.

His brother looked up from the paper he was reading. 'How many more are there to do?' he asked.

'Fourteen,' answered Paul, trickling smoke luxuriantly through his nostrils. 'If things remain quiet, I ought to be able to get them finished this week.'

He had been approached by a well-known firm of publishers to write a book on unsolved crimes with his own suggested solutions. The idea had appealed to him, and certainly there were few people more capable of the task, for Paul Rivington had made a life study of criminology.

'I wish something would happen to break the monotony,' Bob grunted as he threw aside the newspaper. 'I'm getting tired of this life of ease.'

Paul Rivington smiled. 'That bus murder threatened at one time to be interesting,' he said. 'But now they've arrested the conductor, it seems to have petered out.'

'Yes, I suppose they've got the right man,' said Bob. 'The whole business seems rummy to me, though.'

'You can depend that the police have got fairly good evidence against Lonsdale,' said his brother, 'or they wouldn't have arrested him. They're always very careful in a murder case.' He broke off as there came a tap on the door and a maid entered.

'There's a young lady wants to see you, sir,' she announced.

Paul took the card she held out on the salver and glanced at the inscription. 'Ask Miss Denver to come up,' he said, and as the maid withdrew, 'Perhaps our quiet time is over.'

Bob grunted. 'Perhaps,' he said. 'Most likely she's lost her pet dog or mislaid her young man.'

'Don't be pessimistic,' said Paul with a smile, 'and don't forget that one of the most dangerous and exciting cases we ever had started with a lady who had lost her pekinese.'

The woman whom the servant presently ushered into the room made Bob swing round in his chair with sudden interest. She was small and slim — dainty was the description that flashed through his mind — and she carried herself with a grace that is not often seen nowadays. Her hair framed a face that was almost a perfect oval, and her head was just sufficiently tilted to add piquancy to her expression. Sally Denver would have merited a second glance even among a crowd of pretty women.

She came into the room with perfect coolness and self-possession. 'It's very good of you to see me, Mr. Rivington,' she said, and the detective, who was a great believer in the character of voices, took an instant liking to this woman's gentle, well-modulated speech. 'I suppose really I should have made an appointment?'

'It's quite unnecessary,' said Paul, pushing forward a chair. 'We only inflict appointments on our clients when we're very busy. Please sit down.' He introduced his brother as Sally sank into the chair he indicated. 'Now what can I do to help you?'

'You've heard of the murder that happened the night before last?' she said. 'The one that was committed on the motor-bus?'

'I've read what the newspapers say about it,' he replied.

'Well, the conductor of the bus is my fiancé,' she said.

Paul looked quickly across at Bob and raised his eyebrows. Sally saw the swift interchange of glances and raised her eyes to his face enquiringly.

'Why did you do that?' she asked.

'Merely because we were talking about the bus murder when you arrived,' answered Paul.

'I'm glad to hear that,' she said coolly. 'If you're already interested in the matter, my task will be less difficult. The police, as you know, have arrested Dick for the murder of this man, and — well, Mr. Rivington, he didn't do it, that's all.'

A slight smile curved Paul's thin lips. 'I see,' he said. 'And I suppose you want me to prove that he didn't?'

She nodded. 'I want you to try,' she corrected him.

'Before I promise anything, I'd like to know a little more about the case. To be quite candid, Miss Denver, the police don't arrest men and charge them with murder unless they have a very good reason, and I see in the papers that the driver has been detained as well. Suppose, before I say definitely whether I will take up the matter or not, you tell me all you know about the affair?'

'I'm willing to do that,' said Sally quickly. 'Though I know very little — except that Dick is innocent. The man who was shot was an American named William Hooper, and he had been dead for not more than a quarter of an hour when the bus arrived at the Barley Mow. If the murder was committed by someone travelling on the bus — and that seems fairly certain — it limits the assassin to one of four persons: Dick,

Harry Mace the driver, and a male and a female passenger.'

'That seems fairly clear,' agreed Paul. 'Were both the passengers on the bus at the time the police doctor says that the murder must have been committed?'

'Nobody seems to be quite certain of that,' answered Sally. 'Although the dead man had been shot no longer than a quarter of an hour before the crime was discovered, the shot could have been fired any time within that period.'

'I see,' said Rivington thoughtfully. 'The other two passengers — the man and the woman — weren't on the bus when it reached the end of the route, were they?'

'No,' answered Sally.

'Where did they alight?' asked the detective.

'The man, who travelled outside, got off at the top of Mason's Hill,' she replied, 'and it seems hardly possible that he could have been the murderer unless the woman was acting in collusion with him, because she didn't get off the bus until after — at Homesdale Road.'

'I presume Lonsdale saw both these

people leave the bus?' said Paul, but she shook her head.

'No,' she answered. 'He didn't see the outside passenger get off, because he was upstairs changing the indication board, and he didn't get down to his platform again until after the bus had passed Homesdale Road and the woman had alighted.'

'Then he didn't see either of them leave the bus?'

'No. When he got downstairs again after changing the boards, Hooper was the only passenger left, and he must have already been dead.' She paused, and Paul rubbed his chin thoughtfully.

'He must have been unless Mace or Lonsdale is guilty,' he said, and then as he saw the look of pain that came to Sally's eyes, 'You mustn't mind me saying that, Miss Denver. If I am to help you, it must be with the strict understanding that I keep an open mind, and that should I discover any evidence against Lonsdale I shall be as free to put it at the disposal of the police as if it were in his favour. In other words, I cannot guarantee to suppress anything I may find out.'

She was silent for a moment, watching the toe of her shoe as it moved restlessly on the carpet, and then she raised her head. 'I'm quite agreeable to that, Mr. Rivington,' she said steadily, 'because I am quite convinced that Dick is innocent.'

'Of course,' Paul went on, 'if I take up the case I shall start my investigation with the assumption that Lonsdale is innocent. Now, is there anything else you have to tell me?'

'Yes.' For the first time her voice faltered, and she seemed to find some difficulty in choosing her words.

'What is it?' he prompted her gently. 'Don't keep anything back.'

'It would be no use even if I wanted to. It will be public property this evening, and anyway the police would tell you. It's just this, Mr. Rivington, and it's the worst piece of evidence against Dick that has come to light. The morning after the murder, that is yesterday, a man mending the road at the corner of Homesdale Road picked up a revolver. It had one empty chamber, and the name, Harry Mace, was scratched on the barrel.'

Rivington's face was very grave as she

finished speaking. 'That's rather bad,' he murmured. 'So that's why they detained Mace too.'

She nodded. 'Yes, I believe that was the reason.'

'You said just now that the finding of this revolver was the worst piece of evidence against Lonsdale. So far as I can see, it seems to point to Mace as the guilty man.'

'I hadn't quite finished,' Sally said quietly. 'The police questioned Mr. Mace about it, but he only said that he couldn't understand how it got there. Afterwards they questioned Dick, and asked him if he knew that Mace possessed a revolver.'

'What did Lonsdale say?' asked the detective as she paused.

'He told the police without any hesitation,' she answered in a low voice, 'that he knew Mr. Mace possessed a revolver because he had borrowed it a few weeks back.'

Paul pursed his lips. 'What did he want to borrow a weapon for?' he asked.

'It was usual for them to walk home together after the bus had been garaged for the night,' she explained, 'but one evening a few weeks ago Mr. Mace had arranged to call on some friends at Keston. Dick was left to walk home alone with the day's takings, and as they were a considerable amount, and the walk is a lonely one, he suggested borrowing Mr. Mace's revolver.'

'What did he do with it after that evening?' asked Paul.

'He placed it in a drawer in his bedroom and forgot all about it.'

'Do Lonsdale and Mace live together then?'

'Yes,' she replied.

'And did Lonsdale tell the police just what you have repeated to me?'

'Yes. You see, when I heard of Dick's trouble, I went to a friend of mine who is a solicitor and got him to go down and see Dick. I wasn't present at the interview, but he told me just what had occurred — that's how I know so much of the detail.'

Paul walked over to the window and back again, his brows knit. 'On the face of things it doesn't look too good, Miss Denver,' he said candidly. 'The police were amply justified in arresting both Lonsdale and Mace. It would've been quite possible for

Lonsdale to have descended from the top of the bus at Homesdale Road, shot Hooper, thrown away the revolver and restarted the bus immediately after.'

'You're not very helpful, are you?' she said, and her voice was a little disappointed.

'You mustn't misunderstand me. I'm merely looking at it from the point of view of the police. I must get their point of view before I can attempt to find a loophole in the evidence. At the present moment I can't see one — though that is not quite truthful. I *can* see one, but it's a very unlikely one.'

'Then you'll take up the case?' said Sally eagerly.

'I'll tell you that after I've been to Bromley and seen Lonsdale himself. I should like to hear the story from his own lips.'

'May I go with you?' she asked.

He shook his head. 'I think it would be better if I went alone. But if you'll give me a telephone number that will find you, I'll ring you up after I've seen him and tell you whether I'm prepared to take the case up or not.'

She gave him a West Central number

which Bob noted down. 'Is there anything else you want to know?' she asked.

'Not at the moment,' he answered

'Then I won't detain you any longer.' She held out her hand. 'Goodbye, Mr. Rivington, and thank you.'

3

Three White Hairs

Detective-Inspector Robin thrust his hands into his pockets, rested his broad shoulders against the mantelpiece, and yawned. 'If only we could find the motive, Maitland,' he grunted, 'the thing would be as clear as daylight. I don't think there's any doubt this fellow Lonsdale shot the old man, and I'm willing to bet that Mace was in on it too.'

Divisional-Inspector Maitland looked across his desk at the Scotland Yard man, and nodded slowly. 'That's my opinion too,' he agreed, 'and as for motive, I've been thinking it over. Probably this man Hooper had a lot of money on him. He may have taken out his wallet during the journey, and Lonsdale, seeing that he was carrying a wad, decided to get hold of it.'

'That's possible. Yes, that's very possible.' The little fat man with the round face and twinkling eyes scratched his chin slowly.

They called him Round Robin at the Yard, for obvious reasons. He had opened his mouth to say something when there came a tap on the door leading from Mainland's office to the charge-room. In answer to the inspector's gruff invitation, a constable appeared.

'There's a Mr. Rivington in the charge-room asking for you, sir,' he announced.

Round Robin looked up quickly. 'Rivington!' he exclaimed. 'Now what the dickens is he doing here?'

'Shall I ask him in?' said Maitland, and at the other's nod he gave order to the constable and the man withdrew.

'Now,' muttered Mr. Robin thoughtfully, 'I wonder if he's come on this bus murder business.'

'Why should he?' said the divisional inspector. 'Doesn't strike me as being the sort of case that would interest him.'

'You never know with Paul Rivington,' said Mr. Robin, shaking his round head. 'He has a trick of appearing on the simplest cases and turning everything inside out.' He stopped abruptly as Paul entered. If Detective-Inspector Robin had been surprised at the presence of Paul, Paul was no less surprised at seeing Mr. Robin.

'Hello!' he greeted. 'I didn't expect to see you here.'

'I didn't expect to see you either,' replied the other. 'How are you, Rivington?' He extended a chubby hand, which Paul gripped. 'What are you doing down here, eh?'

'I'm seeking information.'

'About this bus crime?'

Rivington nodded.

'Why? How do you come into it?'

Paul pulled a chair towards him and sat down. 'If you'll listen for two minutes I'll tell you,' he said.

They listened for two and a half minutes. At the expiration of that time, Paul had given them a résumé of his interview with Sally Denver.

'If you're going to set out to prove that Lonsdale didn't commit this crime,' commented Mr. Robin when Paul had finished, 'you're only wasting your time, Rivington. I was only saying to Maitland before you arrived that the thing is as clear as daylight.'

'There are several shades of daylight,'

answered Paul. 'Anyway, I haven't made up my mind one way or the other. I'm waiting until after I've seen Lonsdale, and that's what I've come for. I want to know if it's possible for me to have a word with him.'

Mr. Robin looked across at the divisional inspector. 'Any objection?' he asked gently.

Maitland shook his head. 'Not me,' he replied. 'If Mr. Rivington wants to see Lonsdale, he can see him, as far as I'm concerned.'

'That's very nice of you, Maitland,' said Paul. 'I promise you I'm not going to butt in and try and snatch the kudos from the official force. Whatever I find out I shall place at your disposal.'

'D'you want to see Lonsdale now?' said the chubby little inspector.

'Yes, I think so,' answered Paul. He rose to his feet as Mr. Robin crossed to the door.

'We're keeping him here until after the inquest,' he explained as he led the way along a stone-flagged passage to the cell.

'When is the inquest?' enquired Rivington.

'Tomorrow morning, ten o'clock. Are you coming?'

'I may,' said Paul. 'As I say, it all depends on my interview with Lonsdale.'

'Well, you won't have long to wait for that,' said Mr. Robin. Stopping outside an iron door, he inserted a key in the lock, turned it, and threw the door open.

Dick Lonsdale was sitting on the truckle bed, and he looked up quickly as they entered. In spite of his unshaven appearance and haggard face, Paul's first impression was that he was extremely good-looking. There was nothing of the conventional criminal in the wide-set blue eyes, crisp fair hair, and thin, firm mouth.

'I've brought a visitor to see you, Lonsdale,' said the inspector. 'This is Mr. Paul Rivington. He's apparently interested in your case and he wants to ask you a few questions.'

Dick rose to his feet. 'How do you do, Mr. Rivington?' he said simply. 'I suppose Sally has been to see you. She said she was going to.'

'She came this morning,' said Paul, shaking the other's outstretched hand, 'and I've come along to hear the story from your own lips.'

'I can only tell you what I've already told the police,' said Dick, 'and if you want me to, I'll go over it again with pleasure.'

'I'd be glad if you would.'

Once more seating himself on the end of the truckle bed, Dick told his story. He told it so clearly that Paul got a very vivid picture of his movements on the fatal part of the journey. What's more, at the end of the recital he had a conviction that the man was speaking truth.

'That seems very clear,' he said when the other had finished speaking. 'Now, will you answer a question or two?' Dick nodded. 'Have you any idea who either of your passengers was?'

'No, they were both strangers to me.'

'Can you describe them?'

Dick gave a detailed description of the woman who had so interested him, but his word picture of the outside passenger was less complete. 'I really didn't take so much notice of him,' he explained, 'but he was an old man, somewhere near sixty I should say. His hair was quite white.'

'Pity you didn't pay more attention to him,' said Paul disappointedly. 'Now, what about Hooper? You're positive you never saw him before he joined the bus at Charing Cross?'

'Positive,' declared Dick. 'He'd certainly never travelled on the Blue Moon before. It's a hobby of mine to take particular notice of the passengers, and since I have a very good memory I should remember if he had.'

Paul Rivington pinched his chin between his thumb and forefinger. 'Tell me about this revolver,' he went on presently. 'Did anyone besides Mace and yourself know that you'd borrowed it?'

'Mrs Mace knew,' replied Dick. 'That's Harry's mother. She was present when we made the arrangement.'

'Nobody else?'

'No, nobody else.'

'When did you last see the weapon?'

Dick considered a moment before replying. 'I think it was about a week ago,' he said, 'but I wouldn't be quite certain. Anyway, it was several days. I put it in a drawer in bedroom in which I kept some old letters and papers, and I remember when I last saw it I made a mental note to return it to Harry.'

'And you can't suggest how it got to the place where it was found?'

'No. I can't understand it at all, unless somebody took it from the drawer.'

Mr. Robin, who was watching Paul keenly, could see nothing in his expression to give him a clue to his thoughts; and when, after a few more questions, Rivington took his leave of the haggard-faced man on the pallet bed, he was still in doubt as to what conclusion the man had come to. He put his curiosity into words as they walked along the stone corridor on the way back to Maitland's office.

'Well, what do you think of it, Rivington?' he asked.

'I'm puzzled,' answered Paul.

'You mean, I suppose,' grunted Mr. Robin, 'that you don't think he's guilty?'

'I mean just that. If he's guilty, he's the biggest fool that was ever born, and he doesn't give me that impression at all.'

'Hm,' grunted the little inspector. 'I suppose you're going to rip things wide open, as usual. And I suppose you want the entire police force to help you?'

A smile twisted the corners of Paul's lips. 'No, not all of it,' he answered. 'I just want a little assistance from you and Maitland.'

'Well, you can have it, you know that,' said Round Robin. 'What is it you want?'

'I want you to let me have a look at that bus.'

'Well, that's easy enough,' said the inspector. 'I'll take you along now, if you like.'

'I should like,' said Rivington.

The way to Menion's Garage took them over the part of the route the Blue Moon had travelled on the night of the murder, and Paul slowed down as he reached the top of Mason's Hill. From there to the Barley Mow he drove at a snail's pace, making mental notes of the distances and trying to visualise Lonsdale's description of all that had happened on that stretch of road two nights ago.

At the Barley Mow he put on speed and soon arrived at Merrion's Garage, where after a swift glance at the outside of the Blue Moon he climbed onto the conductor's platform and made his way down the gangway inside.

'On which seat was Hooper sitting when

he was killed?' he asked.

Mr. Robin pointed it out and Paul made a careful inspection of the immediate vicinity of the seat. He found nothing to reward his search, but on the back of the seat directly behind the fatal one he saw something which attracted his attention and caused him to stoop down quickly.

'What have you found, Rivington?' asked the inspector, suddenly interested.

Without answering, Paul detached two tiny objects that were adhering to the cushion and held them up between his fingers.

Mr. Robin stared at them. 'Why, they're hairs!' he exclaimed disgustedly. 'I thought you'd found something useful.'

'I'm not at all sure that these are not going to prove very useful,' answered Paul, and to the other's surprise, he raised the hairs to his nose and sniffed them.

'What in the world are you doing that for?' asked the inspector.

There was a slight gleam in Paul's eyes as he looked across at his companion. 'Try it yourself,' he said, holding out his hand.

With his red face the picture of bewilderment, Mr. Robin took the white hairs carefully and held them to his nose.

'Smell anything?' asked Paul.

The inspector wrinkled his forehead. 'Yes, a peculiar aromatic smell,' he answered. 'It's very faint, though. What is it?'

'Spirit gum,' answered Paul shortly. 'These hairs never grew naturally. They either came from a wig or a false moustache, and there's still a slight trace of the gum clinging to them.'

The rosy face of Mr. Robin changed, and into his twinkling eyes crept an expression of excitement. 'By Jove, Paul, you mean —'

'I mean,' interrupted Paul, 'that somebody has been inside this bus recently who was either wearing a wig or a false moustache. Keep those hairs carefully, Robin. I think they're going to be very important indeed.'

He turned abruptly, and leaving the interior of the bus began to climb the iron stairway to the top deck. Mr. Robin followed him laboriously, and found him bending over the seat on which the outside male passenger had sat on the night of the murder. For a long time Paul examined it carefully, and presently in the fold of the mackintosh cover he found what he was seeking: another of the white hairs. Comparing it with the two the inspector already had in his possession, he discovered that in colour and texture they were identical.

'I think that's fairly conclusive,' he remarked. 'I shall be very much surprised if the old man who was eccentric enough to travel outside on such a night was an old man at all. The white hair was obviously a disguise.'

Mr. Robin was staring at him, his small mouth wide open, his whole appearance suggesting an overgrown Kewpie doll. 'You know what this means,' he began.

'I know what it suggests.' broke in Paul. 'It suggests that the man who occupied this outside seat was the murderer of William Hooper.'

4

The Man with Red Hair

The first thing Paul did when he got back to the police station was ring up Sally Denver and to tell her that he had decided to take on the case.

'Well,' he said to Maitland when he had hung up, 'let's see what facts we've got in our possession.' He ticked them off, as he spoke, on his fingers. 'Hooper, for some reason we don't know, travelled on the Blue Moon from Charing Cross to the Barley Mow. At some point near Homesdale Road he was shot dead by a person unknown. On the same bus was a man, obviously disguised, and who may or may not have left the bus at the top of Mason's Hill. Those are our facts.'

'Don't forget the revolver with which the crime was committed,' said Round Robin.

'I haven't,' answered Paul. 'Until you hear from the firearms expert, that is not a fact. There's no proof yet that that revolver fired the fatal shot.'

'I'm pretty certain that it did though,' remarked the inspector. 'However, all this talk won't get us anywhere.'

'I quite agree with you,' said Rivington. 'Therefore, if you'll give me Mrs. Mace's address, I'll be getting along there.'

Maitland found the address and gave it to him. After promising that he would look in again during the afternoon, Paul left the police station, and, getting into his car, set off to find Magpie Hall Lane.

After some little difficulty he succeeded in finding it and the house where Mrs. Mace lived. It was a tiny place, spotlessly clean. Mrs. Mace, a stout, pleasant-faced woman, escorted him into the microscopic sitting-room when he had explained the reason for his call.

'I'm sure it's all a dreadful business,' she said as she insisted on his occupying a particularly uncomfortable chair, 'and of course the police have made a mistake. Dick wouldn't kill a fly. Perhaps you'd like a cup of tea, sir? I'm just making one myself.'

'No thank you, Mrs. Mace,' said Paul.

'All I want is to have a little chat with you.'

She sat down opposite him and smoothed her apron with her hands. 'I'm sure I'll do all I can to help you,' she said. 'What was it you wanted to know?'

'My main reason for coming to see you was to ask if you have had any strangers call lately — during the last week, for instance?'

She looked at him with a rather surprised expression. 'I can't think of any —' began Mrs. Mace slowly, and then she stopped with a sudden exclamation. 'Why, yes I can though!' she cried. 'There was the man with red hair. I forgot about him.'

'Red hair!' exclaimed Paul, and his eyes sparkled. 'Come now, Mrs. Mace, this sounds interesting. Tell me all about this man.'

'Well, sir, perhaps you noticed that the house next door is empty?' Paul nodded and she went on: 'The people moved out a fortnight ago. These houses are council houses, and they don't stay empty long because there's generally a queue of people waiting to occupy them. You can understand then that I wasn't surprised when a man came here shortly after the Todmores moved out.'

'How long ago was this?'

'Just about a week, sir,' she answered. 'He came on a motorcycle and left it by the gate outside. He said that the council had notified him of the vacancy and that he and his wife were moving in almost directly. He said he'd come over to take measurements, but in his hurry he'd forgotten the key, and he asked if I'd mind, as the house was the same size, if he took a look over it.'

'And I suppose you said yes?'

'What else could I say, sir? I took him over the downstairs part first and then showed him the bedrooms. He said it was the bedrooms he was most interested in, because he'd have to get some new furniture.'

'And were you with him all the time?' asked Paul as she paused.

'Not quite all the time. He asked me if I had such a thing as a tape measure or a piece of string so that he could get a rough idea of the size of the room. I had a tape measure in the kitchen and I went down and got it for him.'

'Leaving him alone upstairs?' said Rivington. She nodded. 'And do you remember which room he was in when you left him?'

'Yes, sir. It was Dick's room,' she replied, and Paul smiled, for he had expected no other answer. 'He was a very nice man, sir,' she added, 'and most grateful.'

'I'm sure he was,' said Paul dryly. 'And he had a lot to be grateful for!'

'You surely don't think he took the revolver, sir, do you?' Mrs. Mace's rosy face was the picture of dismay.

'I think it's extremely likely,' said Paul. 'Now, apart from his hair, what else can you remember about him? How was he dressed?'

She screwed up her eyes with the effort. 'He had on a leather coat,' she said. 'One of those motoring coats and a cloth cap, and he wore tinted spectacles. That's all I can remember about him, except ...' She hesitated.

'Except what?' he prompted.

'Well, there was a funny smell about him,' she said a little confusedly. 'Like spices.' Paul Rivington sat up quickly. 'I suppose you'd recognise this odour again if you smelt it, Mrs. Mace?'

'Oh yes,' she replied without hesitation.

'Good. Now, is there anything else about this man you can tell me?'

'No, sir. I can't recollect anything.'

'Well, I don't think I need bother you any more for the time being, Mrs. Mace,' said Paul. 'If there's anything else I want to see you about, I know where to find you.'

'I'll be only too pleased to do anything I can, sir, if it's going to help Dick or my boy,' she said as she escorted him down to the front door. 'It's very lonely here without them. I miss them dreadfully.'

'I'm sure you do,' said Paul sympathetically. 'But don't worry, Mrs. Mace. Unless I'm very much mistaken, you'll soon have them back again.'

5

Fresh News

Inspector Robin and Maitland were sitting in the former's office when Paul got back there, and the round-faced little man looked up as Paul came in.

'I have heard,' said Paul without preamble, 'of a man who visited the Maces' house — a red-haired man, whose hair smelt strongly of spirit gum!'

Two faces stared at him incredulously. 'What's that?' spluttered Mr. Robin, almost incoherent with surprise.

Paul gave an account of his interview with Mrs. Mace, and Round Robin's expression grew more and more interested as he proceeded. 'It certainly looks as if there was something in your idea after all,' he muttered when Paul had finished. 'But why in the world should the man have chosen to disguise himself with a red wig, of all colours? He must have known that it would stick in anybody's memory.'

'I think it was a particularly clever move,' said Paul. 'It proves we're dealing with a man of intelligence. Do you realise that nobody ever remembers anything about red-headed people except that they've got red hair? Our murderer knew that if anyone set enquiries on foot for him, they'd look for a red-headed man. He never expected that we'd find the hairs on the bus and recognise the odour of spirit gum that clung to them, any more than he expected that Mrs. Mace would notice that odour and mention it to me.'

'Yes, I see that.' Mr. Robin nodded quickly. 'Oh, and we've got some news as well, Paul. While you were away I had a message from the Yard. The firearms experts have reported on the revolver and the bullet.'

'What have they got to say?'

'What I expected them to say. The bullet was fired from that particular weapon. It was what they said afterward that I didn't expect.'

'What was that?'

'Well, they said that from certain marks

on the barrel, they've ascertained that the weapon had been fitted with a silencer.'

Paul's eyes narrowed. 'That's interesting — very interesting,' he murmured. 'That explains why neither Mace nor Lonsdale heard the shot. It's also very suggestive.'

'In what way is it suggestive?' asked Maitland.

'Silencers for pistols aren't very common in this country,' answered Paul. 'One associates them more with America.'

'Well?' said Round Robin as Paul paused thoughtfully.

'Well,' Paul continued, 'Hooper was an American. I would suggest, therefore, that you have an enquiry made into Hooper's past. Something maybe learned from it that will help.'

'It's already being done,' said Round Robin. 'We cabled America yesterday.'

'Hadn't he any friends in this country?' asked Rivington. 'I tell you what I'm most anxious to know. Why did he make that journey on Blue Moon? I think that's got a big bearing on the crime.'

'So far as we can find out, he hadn't any friends in England at all,' said the inspector.

'He hadn't been over here very long, and at the Palace Hotel they say that he was a very quiet, reserved old gentleman who never had any visitors and seldom went out.'

'His solicitors couldn't help either, Mr. Rivington,' remarked the divisional inspector. 'They appear to know as little about him as anybody.'

'Who are his solicitors?' asked Paul.

'Messrs. Sampson and Renning of Shortes Gardens,' answered Mr. Robin. 'At least, they're the London agents for his solicitors in New York.'

'I suppose you've interviewed them?' said Paul.

The inspector nodded. 'Oh, yes. At least, I saw their managing clerk. A fellow called Hallows. Old Renning was out when I called.'

'And he could tell you nothing?'

'Nothing at all,' answered Round Robin gloomily.

Paul frowned. 'It's the motive we've got to look for,' he muttered. 'If only we could find that, we'd have something to work on.' He looked up suddenly. 'Did Hooper leave a will?'

'That's the first thing I asked the solicitors,' answered Robin, 'and they said they didn't know. They've cabled over to the New York firm asking them. They did tell me, though, that Hooper was worth something like two and a half million.'

Paul Rivington pursed his lips in a silent whistle. 'Much as that, eh? Quite a respectable sum to tempt a person to do murder, Robin. I'd like to know who inherits the money.'

'I've no doubt the New York —' began Mr. Robin, but he broke off as the telephone rang insistently.

Maitland picked up the receiver and listened. 'Yes, he's here sir,' he said after a pause. 'Hold on, will you?' He looked across at the little inspector. 'The Yard wants to speak to you.'

Mr. Robin took the receiver from his hand and held it to his ear. 'Hello!' he said gently. 'Yes, speaking. Oh, yes, sir.' His voice changed suddenly, and his round rosy face became animated. 'Would you mind repeating that, sir?'

Watching, Paul saw him flush with excitement as he listened to the message coming over the wire.

'I'll be coming back at once, sir,' he ended, and then he turned to Paul with a peculiar look in his eyes. 'That was Chief-Inspector Caler,' he said. 'Messrs. Sampson and Renning have just rung up the Yard —' He stopped to clear his throat.

'Well?' said Paul impatiently.

'Well,' said Round Robin, 'they've supplied us with the motive. Hooper did leave a will, and they've just found it. It was made a week ago, and it leaves all his money to Richard Lonsdale!'

6

The Second Name

It was Paul who first broke the silence that followed. 'How is it that the solicitors have taken such a long time to acquaint you with the fact that this will existed?' he asked.

'I don't know.' Mr. Robin shook his head. 'I suppose they'd only just found it.'

'I wonder *how* they found it,' murmured Paul. 'It couldn't have been put in their charge, or they would've known about it sooner. I should very much like to know how it is that they've only just heard of it.'

'Does it matter?' enquired the inspector. 'The main thing is that the will exists, and that it supplies us with the thing we were looking for — the motive for the murder.'

'My God, yes!' exclaimed Maitland, bringing his big fist down on his desk with a bang. 'It pretty well clinches the matter, so far as Lonsdale is concerned.'

Paul raised his eyebrows, and the fingers

of his right hand caressed the little moustache that lay along his upper lip. 'I want to get back to town as soon as possible,' he said. 'But before I go, I'd like to see how Lonsdale receives the news that he's Hooper's heir. Do you think it would be possible to tell him now?'

The inspector pursed his lips, hesitated, and looked at Maitland.

'He'll have to know sooner or later,' went on Paul, 'so I can't see that it will make any difference.'

'All right,' said Mr. Robin, 'come along.' He picked up the key which he had put down on the divisional inspector's desk after their return from their previous visit, and once more they made their way along to the cell.

Dick looked rather surprised to see them. Apparently he had been asleep, for he was lying on the truckle bed full length when they entered, and he struggled up, blinking.

Mr. Robin came straight to the point. 'Some news has just come through, Lonsdale,' he said, 'which we thought you ought to know at once. William Hooper's solicitors have discovered a will in which he leaves all his property to you.'

Never in his life had Paul seen such an expression of surprise as that which came into the face of the young man on the truckle bed. His mouth gaped open foolishly, and he stared at the stout inspector as though he had suddenly changed into an animal in front of his eyes. For nearly two whole minutes he remained silently stupefied, and then he found his voice.

'To me?' he stammered. 'There must be some mistake.'

'No, it's perfectly true,' said Paul. 'We've just had the news over the telephone.'

'But why?' Dick's voice was shrill with incredulity. 'Why should a complete stranger leave me his money?'

'Are you sure that he was a complete stranger?' put in the inspector sharply.

'Sure? Of course I'm sure,' answered Dick. 'I told you before, and can only repeat it — I never saw William Hooper in my life until I got on the bus at Charing Cross on the night he was killed.'

'Well, if that's the case,' said Round Robin, 'it seems funny to me that he should've made a will in your favour.'

'It's incredible,' said Dick. 'I'm certain that there must be some mistake.'

'We were hoping,' said Paul, watching him keenly, 'that you'd be able to suggest some reason why Hooper should've made a will in your favour.'

'I only wish I could, Mr. Rivington,' said Dick with a helpless gesture. 'But I'm as much bewildered as you are. I can't even believe it's true.'

'It's true enough,' said Round Robin. 'And I need hardly tell you, Lonsdale, that this makes things look very black against you.'

'I realise that.' Dick nodded, and a troubled expression came into his face. 'I can see exactly how it must look to you, and how it will look to other people, but I can only reiterate that I cannot explain it, and that I had no hand whatever in the death of the poor old gentleman.'

'I believe you, Lonsdale,' said Rivington. 'Now I want you to do something. I want you to try and remember anything in your life — even during your boyhood — that might throw some light on this will business. Perhaps some relation of yours knew

Hooper and rendered him a service.'

Dick smiled. 'I've no relations living,' he answered, 'so it would be very difficult to find that out. But it's not an impossible idea, because I was born in America.'

'Oh, were you?' said Paul quickly. 'I never knew that.'

'You never said so,' broke in Mr. Robin.

'Didn't I?' answered Dick. 'I suppose I took it for granted that you knew. I don't remember anything about it because we came to England, my mother and I, when I was quite a child.'

'This is most important,' said Paul. 'It forms a connecting link — rather vague perhaps — between yourself and Hooper.'

'It certainly does,' remarked the inspector, 'and I'm not surprised you forgot to mention it, Lonsdale.'

Dick flushed. 'What do you mean —?' he began hotly, but Paul interposed.

'From the point of view of the police,' he said hastily, 'you must see that the fact that you were born in America is very damaging; that's what Inspector Robin means.'

'I can assure you that I never thought of wilfully suppressing the fact,' said Dick.

'I'm sure you didn't,' answered Paul. 'Were you ever made a British subject?'

'There was no need, Mr. Rivington,' replied Dick. 'Both my parents were British. They were only in America on a visit when I was born.'

'I see,' said the detective. 'I suppose that Richard Lonsdale is your full name?'

'Well, no, it isn't,' said Lonsdale, looking rather surprised at the question. 'My full name is Richard Warne Lonsdale, but I never use the 'Warne'.'

After a few more questions Paul took his leave, offering to drive Mr. Robin up to town and drop him at the Yard, a suggestion which the inspector gratefully accepted.

All through the journey a vague memory disturbed Paul, and over and over in his mind he repeated 'Richard Warne Lonsdale, Richard Warne Lonsdale' until the words blended with the rhythm of the engine. But the elusive memory which the sound of those names in juxtaposition had awakened refused to emerge from the shadows that shrouded it.

7

The Reason

When Paul was shown into the private office of Mr. Renning (Messrs. Sampson and Renning, Solicitors), a grey-haired man who had been seated behind a great desk littered with books and papers rose to his feet. 'Good morning, Mr. Rivington,' he greeted. 'I am acquainted with your name, and I presume that you have come to see me with regard to the murder of poor Hooper.'

'That is quite correct,' answered the detective.

'I was sure it couldn't be about anything else,' said the lawyer, 'since we are not criminal lawyers.' He waved his hand towards a chair and, when Paul had seated himself, sat down in a padded chair behind the desk.

'The death of Hooper has been a great shock to me, as you can imagine,' said Mr. Renning, playing with a pair of gold pince-nez which he wore on the end of a black cord, 'and the whole thing is most sad — most sad. I presume that you've called to see me with regard to this will?'

'Partly,' said Paul, 'and also in the hope that you'll be able to give me some further information about Mr. Hooper.'

'I'm afraid I know very little about the deceased,' said Mr. Renning, shaking his head. 'What little we did know concerning him my managing clerk, Mr. Hallows, told the police when they called.'

'Have you any idea why Mr. Hooper made this will leaving the money to a stranger?'

'No, I must confess that ever since I saw the will I have puzzled over that,' said the lawyer.

'Did you draw the will up yourself?'

'No.' Mr. Renning raised his glasses and peered at them as though seeking information. 'I was completely unaware of its existence until Mr. Hallows brought it to me, and then I immediately communicated its contents to Scotland Yard.'

'How was it,' said Paul, 'that there was so much delay in disclosing its contents?'

'There was no delay as far as we were

concerned,' said the lawyer. 'The will was only discovered this morning.'

'How was that? Where was it found, then?'

'In a safe deposit. Apparently Mr. Hooper had rented a safe in Fetter Lane, and this morning the manager of the safe deposit rang us up and informed us of the fact. Mr. Hallows went along at once and found the will.'

'Were there any other documents?'

'No,' replied the lawyer. 'There was a very large sum of money, but that was all.'

'I suppose there's no doubt that the will is genuine?' queried Paul.

'Oh, no, not the slightest. It was properly executed, and witnessed by two of the staff at the Palace Hotel. The signature is beyond dispute.'

'When was it made?'

'It's dated the fourteenth. Nine days ago.'

'And you've no idea why Hooper should have left his money to Lonsdale?'

'None at all. I have never heard his name mentioned.'

'The whole thing is most extraordinary,' said Paul, frowning. 'I suppose your partner,

Mr. Sampson, knows nothing either?'

A dry smile crinkled the lawyer's thin face. 'There is no Mr. Sampson,' he answered. 'The last Mr. Sampson connected with this firm died fifty years ago. I am the only surviving member of the firm. My managing clerk, Mr. Hallows — he went down to Bromley, by the way, to identify the body — attends to a great part of our work, and we've discussed the matter of the will at length, but he is as much puzzled about it as I am.'

'Supposing,' said Paul thoughtfully, 'that this will had never been made. Are you aware who would have inherited the money?'

'Yes,' answered the lawyer. 'It would've gone without reserve to Mr. Hooper's stepson, Leslie Craven.'

'Stepson?' Paul looked up quickly. 'Did Mr. Hooper marry a widow, then?' The lawyer nodded. 'Have you seen this stepson?'

'No,' answered Mr. Renning. 'I understand he's in America.'

'I see.' Paul rubbed his chin. 'I presume that if Richard Lonsdale were found guilty of this murder and suffered the penalty, having no next of kin, the money would revert to this man, Craven?'

'Most certainly,' agreed the other.

'I must apologise for all these questions, Mr. Renning,' said the Paul, 'but it is only by delving that one can hope to light on something that might prove to be a clue to the solution of the mystery.'

Mr. Renning raised his rather thin eyebrows. 'I had no idea that there was any mystery to solve, Mr. Rivington,' he said. 'I was under the impression that the police had got their man.'

'If you mean Lonsdale,' replied Paul, 'which of course you do, I'll tell you in confidence that although the police seem satisfied as to his guilt, I personally am by no means sure they're right.'

There was no doubt as to the surprise his words caused. Mr. Renning dropped the gold glasses he had been fiddling with throughout the interview, and his impassive face was the picture of amazement. 'Dear me, Mr. Rivington,' he said, 'you astonish me. I thought there was no doubt, no doubt at all. May I ask on what you base your belief in Lonsdale's innocence?'

'On several things,' replied Paul. 'Quite insignificant in themselves, but less so when you consider them *en masse*.' He gave a brief account of his discoveries and conclusions of the day, and the lawyer listened attentively.

'I must admit,' he said when Paul had finished, 'that you have a certain amount of reason for your doubt of Lonsdale's guilt, athough I think you'll have great difficulty in discovering the entity of this red-haired man.'

'I anticipate that,' said Paul, and then: 'I should very much like to know for certain whether Mr. Hooper's stepson is really in America.'

Mr. Renning directed a shrewd glance at him from his rather small, beady eyes. 'Why do you say that?' he asked quickly.

'I was thinking it must be a very unpleasant experience to feel a million pounds or more slip from one's grasp.'

'You surely don't imagine that Mr. Craven had anything to do with the crime?'

'If Lonsdale didn't commit the murder, Mr. Renning,' said Paul slowly, 'somebody did, and at the same time did his best to throw suspicion on Lonsdale. All I'm suggesting is that it would be very convenient for this man Craven if Lonsdale were hanged. It would put two and a half million in his pocket.'

Mr. Renning had opened his mouth to reply when the door opened and a tall, thin man entered. He was neatly, almost fastidiously dressed, and his face radiated vitality. He had evidently just come in from the street, for he carried his hat in his hand and was still wearing his gloves.

'I'm sorry,' he said apologetically as he caught sight of Paul. 'The boy didn't tell me you were engaged.'

'It's all right, Mr. Hallows,' said Mr. Renning. 'This is Mr. Rivington, who came to see me about the death of poor Hooper. This is my managing clerk, Mr. Hallows, Mr. Rivington.'

'I'm delighted to meet you, Mr. Rivington,' said Hallows, pulling the glove off his right hand and advancing into the room.

'Hallows is a keen student of crime,' said the lawyer with a smile. 'In fact, I think he would prefer it if we had a criminal

57

practice.'

'I should,' agreed Hallows. 'That's why I am so interested in this Hooper business. But how do you come into it, Mr. Rivington? I shouldn't have thought it was a case for you. Too simple.'

'I'm rather inclined to think that it's not so simple as everybody imagines,' replied Paul, and Hallows opened his eyes.

'Mr. Rivington doesn't think Lonsdale is guilty after all,' remarked the lawyer.

'Not guilty?' exclaimed Hallows. 'Well, you've surprised me. I shouldn't have thought there was any doubt, particularly after the finding of the will.'

'Mr. Rivington seems to think that Leslie Craven may have had something to do with the murder of his stepfather,' said Mr. Renning.

Hallows whistled, and the expression on his face became curiously eager. 'By Jove!' he exclaimed. 'I never thought of that.' He wrinkled his brows. 'But it's quite a feasible suggestion. Of course, with Hooper and Lonsdale out of the way, he'd come into all the money.'

'Have you ever met Mr. Craven?' asked

Rivington.

Hallows shook his head. 'No,' he answered. 'Though I occasionally go to America on business connected with the firm and have, of course, often visited the offices of Mr. Hooper's American solicitors, of which we are the London agents, I never met either Mr. Hooper or Craven there.'

'I hoped you would have met him,' murmured Paul. 'I should very much like to get a description of him.'

'I'll cable to America and see if I can get our people to send over a photograph,' volunteered Hallows.

'That's extremely good of you,' said Paul, 'and at the same time you might enquire if Leslie Craven is still over there.'

'I will,' agreed Hallows, 'and as soon as I get a reply I'll let you know.'

'Thank you. And now I think I've taken up enough of your time.' Paul rose to his feet. He was in the act of shaking hands with Mr. Renning when the telephone rang.

Hallows, with a word of apology, picked up the instrument, and a second later turned to Paul. 'It's for you,' he said.

Paul took the receiver from him, and as

he put it to his ear Mr. Robin's gentle voice came over the wire. 'Is that you, Paul?' he asked.

'Speaking,' replied Paul tersely.

'It's Robin this end,' answered the inspector. 'Can you come along to the Yard at once?'

'I could. Why, what's happened?'

'Something that I think will interest you,' replied Mr. Robin smoothly. 'I've every reason to believe that Richard Lonsdale was William Hooper's son!'

8

Harry Mace's Record

Round Robin was writing a report in his bare and cheerless office when Paul arrived, but he laid down his pen at once as his friend entered, and waved towards a chair. 'You've been quick,' he remarked. 'Sit down and I'll tell you all about the latest development.'

Paul did so, and pulling out his cigarette case selected a cigarette. 'Fire away,' he said briefly.

Mr. Robin took a long, thin, black cigar from his pocket and bit off the end. 'I'd scarcely got back here,' he began, 'when a messenger came up and told me that a woman was in the waiting room who wanted see the officer in charge of the bus murder. She didn't put it exactly like that, but that's what it amounted to. I told him to shoot her along, and she came, bringing with her a small boy aged about six.

At first she was a little incoherent, but by questioning her I managed elicit the fact that she and the child had travelled on the bus on the night of the murder. She had sat next to Hooper and he'd spoken to her. She thought — or rather her husband had made her think — that she ought to come forward and say that he was still alive when she got out at the Coach and Horses.' He paused and applied a light to his cigar.

'What kind of woman was she?' asked Paul.

Mr. Robin's rosy face expanded in a wide smile. 'She wasn't the female passenger that Lonsdale described. When they told me a woman was waiting, I thought it was her, but this was the usual type of working man's wife. Not quite so loquacious as some of them, but still pretty talkative. And when I really got her going, what she said made me sit up and take notice. She told me she'd got on the bus at New Cross Gate and taken the only vacant seat, which was next to Hooper. He spoke to her almost at once, and asked her if she'd like to take the inside place. As the bus was continuously skidding at the time, and she had her little boy on her knee, she accepted his offer. The old gentleman, as she called him, seemed anxious to talk. He asked if the little child was her son. She answered that he was, and he asked her if he was the only child. To cut a long story short, Paul, they seem to have had a long conversation about the woman, her home and the child.'

'Didn't she seem surprised that a perfect stranger should've taken such an interest in her affairs?' asked Paul.

Mr. Robin shook his head. 'I asked her that, and she said he was such a kind old gentleman that she took to him at once.'

'Hm, how does all this lead to the idea that Lonsdale was Hooper's son?' asked Rivington.

'I'm coming to that,' answered Mr. Robin. 'Soon after the bus reached Lewisham Hippodrome, she told Hooper that she was getting out at the next stop, and he took a two-shilling piece out of his pocket and gave it to the kid. When she thanked him, she said he smiled and said, 'I had a little chap like that once, but he was stolen when he was a child. I've found him again now, though, thank God.'

'The woman said that his eyes were all aglow with excitement when he spoke, and when she questioned him further he said, 'My son doesn't know yet that I'm his father, but he's on this bus and I'm going to tell him when we get to the end of the journey.'

'Mrs. Crouch — that's the woman's name, by the way — said that he was just like a child going to a party. Well, that's the story, Paul — and coupling it with this will business, and the fact that the conductor and the driver were the only two people who would be certain to be on the bus at the end of the journey, I don't think there's much doubt as to the identity of Hooper's son, eh?'

'No, I think I agree with you,' said Paul.

'And I don't think there's much doubt now as to who committed the murder,' continued Round Robin complacently. 'I don't think I attach much importance to this 'mysterious stranger who wanders about in different coloured wigs' theory. I'm pretty sure in my own mind that Lonsdale is the fellow.'

'Well, I'm far from sure,' said Paul,

'but we shall see who's right. Supposing I told you that I'd found a man who had a stronger motive for killing Hooper than Lonsdale, what would you think of that?'

'Tell me who he is first,' said Mr. Robin carefully.

Paul recounted his interview with Mr. Renning.

'This man Craven may have had a motive,' remarked the inspector, shaking his head, 'but he certainly didn't have the same opportunity. Before you can even suggest that he shot Hooper, you've got to be able to prove that he was not only in England, but on that bus at the time the old man was killed.'

'I'm not definitely stating that Craven is the killer,' said Paul. 'I'm merely saying that he's certainly worth looking into.'

'Well, I think it's a waste of time,' grunted Round Robin. 'We've — Come in!' He broke off as there came a tap on the door, and a uniformed constable entered. He was carrying an envelope in his band, and this he laid on the desk in front of the inspector.

'From Records, sir,' he announced, and withdrew.

'Excuse me, Paul,' said Mr. Robin, and he opened the envelope. He gave a hurried glance at the contents and his companion saw his face change. He looked across at Paul with a peculiar expression.

'Perhaps this will interest you,' he said. 'Both Lonsdale's and Mace's fingerprints were taken and sent to Records with a request for information. This is their report. So far as Lonsdale is concerned, he's got a clean sheet, but Mace is different.' He picked up a card. 'Listen. Harold Mace. Demobilised sergeant. Royal Field Artillery, Woolwich division. Convicted of burglary, July 15th, 19 —. Sentenced to two years' imprisonment. Description of convicted person: Height — there's no need to read all *that*. What do you think of it, eh?'

'What do *you* think of it?' asked Paul.

'I think it's fishy,' answered Mr. Robin promptly.

'All the same, I don't see how it affects the present case.'

'There's an old saying,' said the inspector rather tritely, 'that you can judge a man by the company he keeps. Mace is an old lag, and he and Lonsdale are as thick as thieves.'

'You're full of cliches this morning, Robin,' said Paul, smiling. 'Anyway, I don't think you're justified in calling Mace an old lag on the strength of one conviction.'

'All the same, it's going to tell with a jury.'

'Such a lot of things tell with a jury that are really of no importance at all,' replied Paul. 'Well, I'm going back to Hampstead to think the whole thing over.'

'I hope you'll let me know if you come to any definite conclusions,' said Round Robin, slightly stressing the word 'definite'. 'Although, as I've already said, I personally think it's a clear enough case. Anyway, I'm going to work on those lines — that Lonsdale is guilty.'

'And I'm going to work on exactly the opposite lines,' replied Paul. 'We'll compare notes as we go along.'

He shook hands with the cherubic little inspector and, leaving Scotland Yard, drove to Hampstead.

Leaving the house that evening after dinner, Paul strolled along towards the Spaniards Road. He walked slowly, for his mind was still occupied with the murder.

He had reached the pond and was contemplating turning back when he heard the staccato rattle of a noisy exhaust, and looking round saw a motorcycle speeding towards him. As it drew level with him, the muffled figure crouching over the handlebars moved an arm. Some instinct sent a sudden warning to Paul Rivington's brain and he stepped quickly backwards. As he did so he felt a sharp, searing pain in the upper part of his right arm, and something warm trickled down inside his sleeve. With a muttered exclamation he looked at his coat sleeve. In the upper part of the arm was a small, round hole. The driver of the noisy motorcycle had shot at him as he passed, and but for that quick step backwards, would probably have hit him in a vital place!

9

The Female Passenger

Paul's arm was a little painful when he attended the inquest on William Hooper the following morning. The wound was not a serious one, however, for the bullet had passed clean through the fleshy part of the upper arm, and although it had bled a good deal it had done no very great damage.

The inquest was held in the schoolroom attached to the church, and Paul and Bob arrived just as the proceedings were about to start. As Paul had half-expected, immediately after the evidence of identification had been given by Hallows and the doctor's evidence had been taken, Divisional-Inspector Maitland, on behalf of the police, asked for and was granted a fortnight's adjournment. Paul smiled as he heard the request, for it showed that in spite of Mr. Robin's belief in Lonsdale's guilt, he evidently wanted time to collect further evidence.

He tackled the inspector on this point as they left the school-room together, and Round Robin looked slightly embarrassed. 'Oh, it isn't a question of sufficient evidence,' he answered. 'We've got that, but we haven't had time to sort it all out yet.'

'I'll give you something else to sort out,' said Paul, and he told him about the attempt on his life the previous night.

Mr. Robin was sceptical. 'I don't suppose it has anything to do with this case at all,' he said. 'After all, there must be quite a number of people in London who'd like to see you out of the way.'

'I've no doubt there are,' said Paul, 'but I've got a hunch that that man who fired from the motorcycle was mixed up in this murder business. Don't forget that the man who called on Mrs. Mace came on a motorcycle.'

Round Robin shrugged his shoulders. 'I suppose you've got a fixed idea in your head,' he grunted, 'and it's useless trying to shift it.'

'Quite,' replied Paul calmly. 'And talking of Mrs. Mace, I'd rather like to see her son if I can. It would be rather interesting to hear his version of this burglary business.'

'You can if you want to,' said the inspector. 'I'll have him brought in when we reach the police station.'

The station house was quite close to the school-room where the inquest had been held, and when they got there Paul waited in the large room while the constable went to fetch Harry Mace. He was a stocky man with reddish-brown hair that was so near the colour of his weather-beaten face that it was almost impossible to see where one merged into the other.

Mr. Robin lost no time in preliminaries. 'Mace,' he said, 'you were convicted for burglary in 19 —.'

Mace glanced quickly at Paul and then back again at the inspector. 'That's right,' he replied, 'I was.'

'Did Lonsdale know about it when you and he went into partnership?' asked Mr. Robin.

Mace hesitated before he replied. 'Who are you, and exactly how do you come into this business?'

Briefly Paul explained, and when he

71

had heard the explanation, Mace hesitated no longer. 'All right,' he said, 'I'll answer anything you want to know.'

'That's fine,' said Paul. 'Now tell me how you got mixed up in this burglary business.'

Mace laughed a little bitterly. 'Oh, that's easy. I suppose you know that Lonsdale and I served together during the war? Well, when it was over, I, like a good many others, found myself out of a job. I'd been an engineer, and the firm I'd worked for had amalgamated with a bigger concern and I wasn't wanted. I went from place to place trying to get work, but with no luck. There's no need to go into all the details; I was one of hundreds who went through the same experience. I don't like to think how my mother and I lived during those days. Sometimes we nearly didn't.

'The whole thing reached a crisis when we were faced with a distraint summons for rent, and I was pretty desperate. Neither of us had had anything to eat for a day and a half, and I didn't know what to do. Then I met a chap I'd known before the war. He was an engineer, like myself, and instead of fighting, stayed at home and made money.

72

Although I hated doing it, I asked him if he could help. I won't tell you what he said, because it makes me see red now even to think of it, but I knew where he lived and I made up my mind to burgle his place that night.'

He paused and licked his lips. 'I was such a fine burglar,' he went on, 'that I was caught in the act and got two years. Lonsdale heard of it, and came and looked after my mother while I was inside. He'd been luckier than I and got back his original job. When I came out he told me he'd saved a bit of money and suggested that we should become partners in a bus. I was to do the driving and he was to look after the fares. That's all.' He stopped abruptly.

'I see,' said Paul. 'You don't appear to be a very hardened criminal, Mace. Did you ever hear Lonsdale mention his parents?'

Harry shook his head. 'No,' he answered. 'I believe they both died when he was very young.'

'You never heard him mention the name of Leslie Craven?'

'No, never. I don't think I've ever heard the name before.'

'I think that's all I want to ask you at the moment,' said Paul.

Mace looked enquiringly at Mr. Robin. 'What about you? Is there anything I can tell you?' he asked.

'Not for the moment,' answered the inspector. 'Maybe I'll have a lot to ask you later.' He signalled to the constable, and Mace was led away. 'Well, I hope you learned what you wanted,' he granted when the prisoner had gone. 'Personally, I'm going to have that story of his verified.'

'I think you'll find that he was speaking the truth,' said Paul. 'He gave me that impression.'

'You're too impressionable, that's your trouble. What are you going to do now? I'm going back to town.'

'A very good idea,' replied Paul. 'Bob can drive you back.'

Bob looked up in surprise. 'Aren't you coming too?' he asked.

Paul shook his head. 'Not till later, old chap. I'm going for a walk. I haven't had a lot of exercise lately, and I think a walk will do me good.'

Mr. Robin sniffed. 'Perhaps you'll run

into the man with the red wig,' he said sarcastically.

'Perhaps I shall,' answered Paul good-humouredly. 'If I do, I'll ring you up.'

He filled his pipe, lit it, and set out at an easy pace, allowing his thoughts to come as they would. Presently he found himself mentally repeating the name Leslie Craven over and over again. After a time, subconsciously other names became attached to it. Harry Mace. Dick Lonsdale. Richard Warne Lonsdale. Mace. Lonsdale. Warne. Craven. Round and round in his brain they went, monotonously, sometimes in one order, sometimes another. They seemed to be knocking steadily at the door of his mind, asking to be allowed to enter and tell a story.

He stopped suddenly with an exclamation. 'I believe I've got it!' he said aloud.

The vague memory that had been bothering him suddenly materialised into crystal clearness. Lonsdale. Warne. Craven! There in those three names lay a clue. He conjured up before his eyes a faded newspaper cutting, and the picture was so vivid that he could almost imagine he was reading it. It was an account of the robbery of the Southern Bank of Canada by three men, and the names of the three men had been Lonsdale, Warne, and Craven. It had been exceedingly well-planned, and should have succeeded, but the police had got wind of the affair at the last moment. They had arrived on the scene after the men had committed the robbery and were leaving the bank. There had been a fight, during which Warne and Lonsdale had escaped with the proceeds of the robbery. Craven, however, had been taken, and in the struggle had killed one of the policemen. He had been tried for the crime, found guilty, and hanged.

Paul racked his brains to try and recollect some further details, but without success. He made up his mind, however, to look up that faded newspaper cutting as soon as he got back to Hampstead.

He had reached this decision, and was in the act of climbing over a stile, when his eyes were attracted by a peculiar figure in the field which ran parallel with the one in which he was himself. It was the figure of a woman, and she was walking rapidly down a path that crossed the field at right angles. A thick-set hedge intervened, and but for the fact that he had mounted the stile he would not have been able to see her at all. But now as he looked he felt a sudden quickening of his pulse, and into his mind came Dick Lonsdale's description of the female passenger who was supposed to have left the bus at Homesdale Road.

'She was tall, gaunt, and angular, with huge feet encased in hobnail boots, and she carried in her hand a knotted ash-stick.'

Paul gazed after the rapidly vanishing figure. The description fitted. Had he by sheer chance found the one person who could supply him with vital information concerning that fatal night?

10

Emily Boulter, Laundress

Paul Rivngton made up his mind to keep the woman in sight. Dropping down on the other side of the stile, he hurried along the field path, trying to find a break in the hedge. He failed to find even the smallest gap, and by the time he had reached the end of the field and found a gate which gave onto the path along which the woman had been walking, she was out of sight.

He came to a halt and looked around him rather irritably. Apparently he had lost her after all. He was trying to make up his mind as to his next move when he noticed a little way down the road, on the opposite side to where he was standing, a small shop which, from the sign on the window, offered tea at a modest price.

Paul felt that a cup of tea was just what he needed at that moment, and crossing the road, he entered the shop. A bright middle-aged woman, obviously the pro-prietor, came forward and took his order, instructed someone in a back room to carry it out, and returned to her place behind the counter. While he waited for his tea, Paul began to draw her into a conversation. He found that this was by no means a difficult matter. After a few preliminary remarks about the weather, he introduced the sub-ject of the bus murder. Immediately she became voluble.

'It's what you'd expect ridin' in one of them pirate buses,' she averred. ''Ow are you to know who the driver or the conduc-tor might be? On the ordinary buses it's different — a man 'as to produce references before he gets his job. But anybody can buy an omnibus and murder defenceless people.'

Paul pretended to agree with her, and then suggested that as there were so many gipsies in the neighbourhood, perhaps one of them had had something to do with the crime.

The woman shook her head. 'No, sir,' she said. 'They're an 'armless lot, really. They might steal something if they got the chance, but they're too scared of the police to do anythin' really bad. An' most of them are better off than you think. Why, one way and another, they make a good living.'

'I saw one this afternoon that I shouldn't like to meet on a dark night,' remarked Paul as he poured out the tea which a girl of about sixteen placed before him. 'She was as big as a guardsman, and carried an ash-stick that looked as though it could do considerable damage to one's skull if its owner were not in a good humour. She was a gaunt, angular woman, and wore a pair of men's hobnail boots. Not at all a prepossessing specimen.'

A smile of amusement crept across the woman's rosy face. 'That sounds like Emily Boulter,' she said. 'But she ain't no gipsy, sir. She's a laundress, and a very good laundress too.'

'I don't think the woman I'm speaking about is a laundress,' said Paul, shaking his head. 'At any rate, I certainly wouldn't trust her with mine.'

'You wouldn't get the chance, sir,' was the reply, 'if it was Emily Boulter. She's worked for certain families in this town for more than thirty years. If any of 'em dies or moves away, she'll take on a fresh customer, but I've 'eard tell there's a waiting list a yard or more long. You see,' she explained, 'there ain't many people now, what with all this chemical cleaning, that'll take the time and trouble to launder like Emily does.'

'She certainly sounds an interesting character. Where does she live?'

'She lives just down the road and round the corner in Prospect Place. There's a notice on 'er front door. But if you're thinkin' of tryin' to get 'er to do any work for you, sir, I'm afraid you'll only be wastin' your time.'

'I wouldn't dream of asking her after what you've told me,' said Paul, and he changed the subject.

He finished his tea, paid the small bill, and, leaving the teashop, set out to find Prospect Place. He had no difficulty in doing this, for it was not a stone's throw away, and about halfway down on the right-hand side in a row of small cottages he saw on one of the doors the brass plate he was seeking. It was so well-polished that the name was almost obliterated by rubbing.

But Paul could just make out the words 'Emily Boulter', and beneath in smaller letters 'Laundress'.

He passed by, taking stock of the house as he did so, and continued to the end of the road. He found that the place was a cul-de-sac blocked at the end by a large garage. The brightness of the day had clouded over. Big rain clouds were piling themselves over the blue of the sky, and even as he began to retrace his steps he felt a splash on the back of one of his hands. It was followed by another and another, and then suddenly down came the rain in earnest.

He opened the small gate of the house in which Miss Emily Boulter presumably laundered, and, walking up the short path, knocked on the door.

'Pull the string and come in,' commanded a deep voice, rather to his astonishment.

Glancing down, Paul noticed a small end of string protruding from the letter-box, and giving it a tug, he heard the click of a latch. He pushed the door, which opened under his hand to reveal a small sitting-room, barely furnished but scrupulously clean, in which the gaunt woman he had seen crossing the field was standing, busy with an iron and an ironing board.

Paul closed the door behind him. 'Good afternoon,' he said.

Emily Boulter looked him up and down in the light of an incandescent gas-burner that projected from the wall. She did so deliberately, the squint in her eyes giving her face a curiously ferocious and malevolent expression. And then without speaking, she went on with her ironing.

Paul felt a little embarrassed and rather like a small boy who had done something wrong and been found out. He cleared his throat and sought an opening. 'I'm very sorry to interrupt you —' he began.

'You're not!' said the strange woman without looking up from her work. 'What do you want?'

He decided that it was useless beating about the bush with this woman. 'I'm a detective,' he said bluntly. 'My name is Rivington, and I'd like you to answer a few questions.'

Emily Boulter carried her iron over to the fireplace, took another from a small gas-ring, and replaced it with the one that was growing cold. Bringing it back to the ironing board, she set it down on the stand and, putting her hands on her hips, regarded him frowningly. 'Young man,' she said, 'sit down and explain yourself!'

Paul sat down.

'Now, what is it you want to know?' she asked. 'And be quick, because I've got a lot of work to do!'

'The first thing I want to know,' said Paul, 'is why, when you were advertised for, you didn't come forward and say what you knew about the murder?'

'What murder?' She stared at him unflinchingly as she put the surprising question to him.

He scrutinised her carefully. She was either completely sincere in her innocence or an excellent actress, and he couldn't make up his mind which. 'The night before last,' he said, speaking very deliberately, 'a man was murdered while travelling in a pirate bus between Charing Cross and the Barley Mow. You must have seen an account of it in the papers.'

'I never have a paper,' she replied simply. 'I can't read!' Her voice held a ring of truth, but her face was still immovable.

'But surely someone must have mentioned the crime to you?' said the amazed Paul.

She shook her head. 'I seldom meet anyone, and I never gossip. I'm far too busy.'

'But you were on the bus — the Blue Moon — the night before last?' he said.

'I got on a bus, yes,' she replied, 'but whether it was called the Blue Moon or not I couldn't tell you. I went to Lewisham shopping, and I went to a picture theatre after.'

'And you got on the bus at the Obelisk?'

'That's right.'

'After the bus left Bromley Station, how many passengers were there inside?'

'Me, and an old man who was sitting up near the front,' she answered without hesitation.

'What was he like?'

'I only saw his back. I wouldn't know him again if I saw him.'

'You won't see him again,' said Paul quietly. 'He was the man who was killed.'

The rain was pattering on the windows,

and the wind, which had suddenly risen, rattled the old frames and, creeping in through the chinks, fluttered the gas mantle, causing the flame to flicker. It threw queer shadows across the face of Emily Boulter with its squinting eyes, and made her look like some evil witch of old as her deep harsh voice asked: 'Who killed him? The conductor or the man with the onyx ring?'

11

The Onyx Ring

In that shabbily furnished room with its grotesque shadows, a silence fell.

'I think,' Paul said, looking steadily at the strange woman opposite him, 'that it was the man with the onyx ring.'

She gave a quick, sharp nod. 'I think you're right,' she replied with conviction.

He leaned forward eagerly. 'Tell me why you think that?' he said.

'Because,' said Emily Boulter, 'a man who was about to do murder wouldn't have been so interested in my feet as that conductor was!'

Paul smiled as she lifted the iron from the gas-ring and continued her work.

'That is rather a pertinent observation,' he said. 'Now will you tell me all you can concerning this man who wore the onyx ring?'

She turned over the flimsy garment she

was carefully ironing before replying. 'It's little enough. I only saw him for a few minutes. As like as not I shouldn't have noticed him at all, only I thought he must be soft to ride outside on such a night.'

'What was he like?' asked Paul as she paused.

'His face was rather pale,' she replied, 'and he had on a soft hat pulled down over his eyes. There was a patch of white hair showing at one side, and his eyebrows were white and rather bushy. Instead of getting off the bus as I thought, he made to go inside, and it was then that I saw the ring.'

'Which finger was it on?'

'The wedding finger.'

'What kind of ring was it?'

'It was a funny ring; that's what made me notice it. The gold band was broad and the stone was cut in the shape of a cross.'

'Then it shouldn't be difficult to recognise,' murmured Paul.

'You couldn't mistake it.'

'Did you notice what the old man did when he got inside?'

'He sat down on the opposite side of the gangway to the old gentleman,' she answered, 'and then the bell rang twice and I got off the bus just as it started, and hurried home.'

'You didn't look back?'

She shook her head. 'No, it was as much as I could do to force my way along against the wind,' she said.

He was silent, and the woman went on with her ironing as though he wasn't in the room at all.

He had established one important point. The outside passenger had been alone with Hooper during the run from Mason's Hill to Homesdale Road. Sufficient time for him to have committed the crime and to spare.

'There's nothing else you can think of about this man's appearance that would be likely to help in tracing him?' he said at length.

She thought for some time before she answered. 'No,' she said, and then: 'Except that as he brushed past me to go inside, I noticed a funny smell like methylated spirit.'

Paul's eyes sparkled. 'You're sure of that?' he asked eagerly.

She nodded. 'Yes. At first I thought he'd been drinking, then I was certain it wasn't that kind of smell at all. Though it was like some kind of spirit.'

Paul rose to his feet. 'You've been a great help,' he said, holding out his hand, 'and now I won't disturb you any longer. Perhaps if there's anything else I wish to ask you, I may come again?'

Emily Boulter shook his hand with a grip that was like a man's. 'Come whenever you want to,' she said. 'If ever you think of living in Bromley, I'll do your washing for you!'

He took his departure, feeling rather as he might have felt had the King bestowed a decoration on him at Buckingham Palace.

When he got to Hampstead, he searched through his books of press cuttings for the account of the robbery of the Southern Bank of Canada. He had some little difficulty in finding it, but eventually ran it to earth in a volume marked 'Miscellaneous'. The cutting was yellow with age, and below it was another referring to the same matter. He carried the book over to the chair and settled himself comfortably.

Both paragraphs were very short. The first one was a brief account of the robbery and the shooting of the police officer, and

Paul found that his memory had not been at fault. Craven had been caught and arrested, but the other two, Warne and Lonsdale, had got away — and got away with the money — two hundred thousand dollars. The second cutting gave an account of Craven's execution. The man had apparently gone to his death swearing vengeance against his two associates. There was nothing to say whether Warne and Lonsdale had ever been caught, or whether the money had ever been recovered.

One paragraph, however, held his interest. It referred to a visit paid to Craven by his son three days before the execution. 'Just as it was time for the condemned man's son to leave him,' it ran, 'Craven took from his finger a ring which he had worn throughout the trial. 'Take this,' he said to his son. 'It's all I have to leave you'.'

Paul Rivington let the book rest open on his knees and stared up at the ceiling. Was this ring that Craven had given the son the same ring that Emily Boulter had seen on the finger of the outside passenger? Although in the paragraph he had just read there was no description of it, it seemed more than probable. The coincidence that there were two rings seemed rather too great to be given credence. And if there was only one ring — if that ring which Craven had given to his son during his last few hours alive were an onyx in the shape of a cross — then the natural conclusion was that the man on the bus was Leslie Craven.

12

News from America

It was nine o'clock exactly next morning when Paul left the house, and finding a taxi, was driven to Scotland Yard.

Round Robin was hanging up his hat and coat in his office when Paul was announced, and he looked round with surprise on his red, cheery face. 'Hello!' he greeted. 'You're an early visitor. What's the matter — insomnia?'

'I suppose you mean that this would be a good place to come if I suffered from that complaint!' retorted Paul. 'No. The fact is, Robin, I've got news.'

The inspector crossed over to his desk and settled himself in his chair. 'About this bus business, I suppose?' he said with his head to one side. 'What have you got hold of now? More men with wigs?'

'No, a man with a ring this time,' said Paul, smiling. 'If you sit still and listen, I'll tell you all about it.'

Mr. Robin closed his eyes and heaved a weary sigh of resignation. 'Carry on,' he said weakly.

Paul carried on. As he proceeded, Mr. Robin's eyes grew wider and wider. 'By Jove, Paul!' he exclaimed. 'This story of yours puts a different complexion on things. Quite a different complexion. You know, I'm beginning to believe there may be something in your theory after all.'

'I'm sure that I'm on the right track, Robin,' said Paul with conviction. 'It's utterly impossible that all these facts are coincidences. I'm sure that the man who killed Hooper is Leslie Craven.'

'It looks as if you were right,' said Mr. Robin with a rueful face. 'I'm afraid I was a bit stubborn, Paul, but I really did think you were barking up the wrong tree.'

'I wasn't definitely sure myself. Now, it strikes me at once that if you notified all stations and patrols and had the description of the ring circulated in the *Police Gazette*, we might get results.'

'I'll have all that done, of course,' said Mr. Robin, but his tone was somewhat dubious. He drew a pad towards him and made a note.

'They have been known to come off,' remarked Paul. 'And here's another thing.' He took three sheets of manuscript he had written that morning from his pocket. 'Here are some facts I'd like to know about the robbery of the Southern Bank of Canada, and also about Leslie Craven, that you may be able to get for me.'

The little inspector glanced quickly at the closely written pages. 'I'll cable to the Canadian Police and to America at once,' he said. 'I'll also see if I can't get a telegraphed picture of this man Craven. That would help.'

Paul shook his head. 'I'm doubtful about the photograph being any good. Craven will almost surely be disguised.'

'Yes, I suppose you're right.' Mr. Robin frowned. 'It's going to be a dashed difficult business, Paul, and there's no getting away from it.' He reached out and picked up a telephone receiver as the bell shrilled. 'Hello! Yes, he's here — hold on!' He turned to Paul. 'Man called Hallows wants to speak to you,' he said, pushing the instrument across the desk.

Paul put the receiver to his ear, and in reply to his 'Rivington speaking' the voice of Sampson and Renning's managing clerk came over the wire.

'I tried to ring you up at your house, Mr. Rivington,' said Edgar Hallows, 'but your brother told me that I should probably find you at Scotland Yard. I've had a reply to our cable to America.'

'Oh, yes,' said Paul quickly. 'What do they say?'

'Leslie Craven left New York six months ago.'

Paul's eyes gleamed. 'Have they any idea where he went?'

'No,' answered the managing clerk, 'but they think his intention was to come to England.'

'What's he got to say?' asked Mr. Robin as his friend hung up the receiver.

Paul gave him the gist of the conversation.

'So Craven's not in America, eh?' grunted Round Robin. 'Looks as if you were right after all, Paul.'

The following afternoon a message came through to Detective-Inspector Robin, sitting in his office at Scotland Yard, which he promptly relayed to Paul Rivington.

The man with the onyx ring had been found, and in the last place in the world that either of them would have ever expected!

13

'Z4'

Paul Rivington did not go straight home when he left Scotland Yard. Strolling up Whitehall, he crossed Trafalgar Square and turned into the Mall. Making his way at a leisurely pace, he passed Buckingham Palace, and presently arrived at Victoria. Negotiating the maze of side streets that lie at the back of the station, he turned into one that was even dingier and less inviting than its fellows, and halfway along this he entered a shabby-looking house that bore over its fascia the name 'Avenue Hotel'.

A waiter limping painfully, and dressed in a suit that was rapidly turning green where it was not splashed with grease, stopped as he passed from dining-room to kitchen and asked Paul if he was looking for anyone.

'Mr. Marie in?' asked Rivington.

The man nodded. 'Yes, sir,' he said in a dull, lifeless voice that matched his pale, tired, and wizened face. "'E's in the back.'

'Tell him that Mr. Rivington would like to see him, will you?' said Paul, and the waiter shuffled away.

In less than half a minute, the fat proprietor of this depressing establishment came hurrying to the hall, his round face beaming. 'This is an unexpected pleasure, Mr. Rivington,' he exclaimed, in a high, wheezy voice. 'Is this a friendly visit or business?'

'Business,' said Paul laconically.

The stout man looked quickly about the deserted hall, and rubbed his chin with the top joint of his thumb. 'Better come up into the office,' he said in a hoarse whisper. 'It'll be more private.'

He led the way up the staircase, warning Paul to mind the holes in the carpet; and, walking down the corridor on the second landing, he unlocked a door at the end. Holding it open, he stood aside for Paul to enter; and then, coming in himself, he closed and relocked the door. The contrast between this room and the rest of the hotel was remarkable. It was furnished so well as to be almost luxuriant.

Paul, who had been to this apartment many times but never lost interest in it, crossed to a massive easy chair and dropped into its yielding embrace. 'You do yourself very proud, don't you, Marie,' he remarked quizzically.

Mr. Marie beamed. 'I like to live in pleasant surroundings,' he said. 'Yes, I like to live in pleasant surroundings, and I am not exactly poor, so why not, why not?'

Paul leaned back and surveyed this fat, commonplace little man, who was known in a certain high official's office near Whitehall as 'Z4', and wondered. In spite of his appearance he was able to speak seven languages fluently and two others passably, was a past master at disguise, and had done more for his country during the war than any other three men put together; and had, moreover, done it in the dark, working unknown to anybody except the department that employed him.

'I want some information,' said Paul. 'Thirty-five years ago, three men broke into the Southern Bank of Canada ...'

★   ★   ★

It was in the middle of breakfast the next morning that the message came through from Round Robin, and Paul Rivington's face when he heard what the Scotland Yard man had to say was a study.

'What is it?' asked his brother when Paul hung up the receiver. 'News?'

'It's news all right,' answered Paul with knitted brows. 'They've found the man with the onyx ring.'

Bob's eyes lit up. 'Where?' he demanded eagerly.

'In a cell at Buckley Police Station!' replied Paul. 'He's been there twelve days on a charge of drunkenness while driving, and assaulting a police officer.'

'What!' exclaimed his brother. 'There must be some mistake. It can't be the same man.'

Paul looked at him curiously. 'Then it's our mistake, old chap,' he said. 'The name of the man wearing that ring is Leslie Craven!'

14

The Setback

The entire population of the as yet unspoilt village of Buckley, in Kent, is under three hundred. To this miniature Garden of Eden — in which the Serpent had not yet made an appearance — came Paul Rivington, his brother, and Inspector Robin. They came in Paul's long-bonneted car in the early afternoon, and pulled up before the small police station — the only eyesore in the village, for it had been newly built in glaring mustard-coloured brick and imitation stone, and bore the inevitable blue lamp over the entrance.

In the green-distempered charge-room they found a bucolic sergeant laboriously making entries in a large ledger, and to him they introduced themselves and asked for Inspector Chuff.

''E's out,' said the sergeant, regarding them with a fishy stare. ''E's gorn to see

Mr. Newton about 'is cow.'

'How long is he likely to be?' asked Paul.

The sergeant shook his red head and scratched the back of his ear with the end of his penholder. 'Couldn't say,' he replied after much thought.

'Well, I suppose we can't do anything until Inspector Chuff returns,' Paul remarked, suppressing a smile at Round Robin's obvious ill temper. 'So we may as well wait as patiently as possible.' He glanced round, found a chair and sat down.

'You've come about this feller with the ring, ain't yer?' said the sergeant conversationally, and Round Robin nodded. 'Pretty desperate chap, 'e is. Poor old Dibble's still abed with a cracked skull.'

Paul gathered that Dibble was the officer who had been assaulted, and after one or two questions succeeded in extracting the whole story from the sergeant. Leslie Craven had apparently crashed into the signpost at the end of the village, and the accident had been witnessed by Constable Dibble, who had been passing on his bicycle. Dibble had gone to investigate, and found that Craven was considerably the worse for drink. He had, in the execution of his duty, attempted to arrest the man, but Craven had resisted. In fact, to use the sergeant's own expression, ''E fought like the devil,' ending by coshing Constable Dibble with a spanner. At this moment Inspector Chuff had appeared on the scene, and after great difficulty had succeeded in taking the still-fighting Craven to the police station. This, shorn of many interpolated details, was the story told by the desk sergeant.

'Why is the man still here?' asked Mr. Robin. 'Hasn't he been brought up before the magistrate for sentencing?'

''E was brought up the next day,' answered the sergeant. 'But 'e was too ill to answer for himself, so the magistrate remanded 'im for a fortnight. 'E's going up again tomorrow.'

He went on with his writing, and the others waited impatiently, Mr. Robin with obvious ill temper. Half an hour went by before Inspector Chuff returned. He was a large man, big-boned and lean, with a face that was seamed and lined. He greeted Round Robin with a nod and held out his hand.

'Glad to meet you,' he said. 'I suppose you've come to see this man, Craven. We saw the description of the ring in Information and phoned the Yard.'

'How long has he been here?' asked Paul.

Chuff wrinkled his forehead. 'Let me see,' he said. 'It was the night after Wilmer's rick caught fire.' He made a rapid calculation on his fingers. 'Twelve days. Today makes the thirteenth.'

'What do you make of it, Paul?' asked Round Robin, coming over to his friend's side.

Paul shook his head. 'I don't know what to make of it,' he declared candidly. 'It's beaten me for the moment.'

'It must be the same man,' muttered Mr. Robin.

'It seems so,' agreed Paul. 'Anyway, let's see him. Perhaps we shall learn something that will help.'

Inspector Chuff was only too willing to take them along to the cells, and leaving Bob in the charge-room they followed him out through a door at the back. He was obviously very proud of the new building, which he informed them had only been put up six months ago. As he led them along the concrete corridor at the end of which were the two cells facing each other, he expatiated on its merits and compared it with its predecessor. 'It was only a converted cottage,' he said. 'We 'ad to keep the prisoners in the scullery, an' they was always getting out. But you wouldn't find better cell accommodation than this anywhere.'

Paul and Robin were forced to agree with him as they saw the massive doors and strong locks. The inspector unlocked the right-hand one and pushed the door open. 'Two people to see you,' he said curtly to the man who was sitting on the edge of the pallet-bed.

He looked up. Paul saw that he was a small man with dark hair that was almost black, and a pallid face on which the marks of dissipation were deeply graven. He was dressed in a crumpled suit of grey hobsack, but had apparently taken the trouble to keep himself shaved, for his face was smooth and without stubble.

'Mr. Craven?' enquired Paul pleasantly.

The man shot him a quick, suspicious glance, and then nodded reluctantly. 'That's my name,' he replied sullenly. 'Who, sir, are you?'

'My name is Paul Rivington, and this is Detective-Inspector Robin from Scotland Yard.' He indicated the chubby-faced inspector.

For a moment a look of dismay crossed the face of the prisoner, and his right hand went up to his lips. It was only for a moment and then it had gone, but Paul had seen it and noted it. The man was afraid of something. What?

'Well, what do you want?' he asked.

'I want to ask you a question or two,' said Paul. 'Firstly, are you any relation to the American millionaire, William Hooper?'

There was a pause, and the light from the little barred window of the cell, catching the gold band of the onyx ring on the third finger of the man's hand, danced and flickered as he pinched at his lips.

'He's my stepfather,' came the grudging reply at length. 'But I don't see what it's got to do with you. Did he send you here?'

'It would be very difficult for him to send anyone anywhere,' said Paul, watching the effects of his words. 'He's dead.'

'What!' Craven sprang to his feet and stood staring at the detective, his face pale and twitching. 'When did he die?'

'He was shot five nights ago on a motor-bus,' answered Paul quietly.

'Good God!' The man before him sank back on the bed and picked at his fingers. 'Is that why you're here?'

'Partly,' said Paul 'I suppose you're aware that until nine days ago you were your step-father's heir?'

'Nine days ago,' said Craven sharply. 'I still am, so far as I know.'

It sounded genuine enough, but Paul could not make up his mind whether he was speaking the truth or not. 'I'm afraid I must disillusion you on that point,' he said. 'A later will was discovered after your step-father's death in which he left everything to a man called Dick Lonsdale, who we have reason to believe is his son.'

'So he succeeded in finding him, did he?' muttered Craven almost to himself, and then he laughed harshly. 'Look here, suppose you tell me all about it? I know nothing about the business at all. I've been cooped up here for twelve and a half days, and I haven't seen a newspaper.'

Paul considered for a moment before he answered. After all, there was no reason why he shouldn't tell Craven all about it. As briefly as possible he did so, and the man listened gravely.

'I'm not surprised you suspected me,' he remarked when Paul ended. 'It seems that I'm rather lucky to have got such a good alibi, and I'm thankful now that for quite another reason I didn't try and get bail, though I've been confoundedly bored. I'd like to know, though, who the chap was that was wearing that ring. You say it was exactly like this one?' He held out his hand.

Paul examined the ring on his finger. 'So far as I can judge from the woman's verbal description,' he said, 'it was exactly like it.'

'Well, it wasn't this one,' said Craven. 'I've been wearing it all the time. The inspector'll tell you that.' He glanced at Chuff, and that official nodded stolidly. 'Besides which, I couldn't get it off if I wanted to without having the band cut.'

This certainly was true. Paul had noticed the ridges of flesh that had grown up on each side of the ring. 'What was the reason why you didn't take advantage of the offer of bail?' he asked.

Craven smiled dryly. 'Because the only person I could have given as a security was my stepfather,' he replied, 'and I didn't want him to know that I'd been locked up for being drunk. He was dead against drink, and I was afraid that if he knew he might alter his will. He threatened to once for the same reason.'

The explanation was a simple one and sounded feasible. Yet Paul felt that there was something wrong somewhere. He did not know what it was. It was just instinct — that instinct that had helped him so many times before. 'You knew then that your stepfather was in England?' he asked.

'Oh yes, I knew that,' said the other readily.

'Did you know why he was here?'

Craven shook his head. 'No. As a matter of fact ...' He hesitated. 'Well, he and I weren't very good friends. There was no quarrel or anything like that, but we just didn't hit it off.'

'I see.' Paul nodded. 'Did your stepfather know that you were here?'

Again the other shook his head. 'No.'

'Why did you come over?'

There was a perceptible pause before he got a reply to this question. 'I came over because of a woman,' said Craven at last. 'But I don't want to drag her into it. I might as well tell you that it was a woman of whom my stepfather strongly disapproved.'

Paul put one or two more questions which Craven answered openly and without apparent flurry, and then accompanied by Mr. Robin and Inspector Chuff he went back to the charge-room.

'Well, that's that,' said Round Robin. 'That lets Craven out. He couldn't have been in two places at once.'

15

Attempted Murder

The finding of Leslie Crane in the police station at Buckley dealt a severe blow to Paul's theory. In fact it smashed it completely. The man's alibi was cast-iron and allowed no loophole. At the time that William Hooper had been shot on the Blue Moon, Craven had been securely locked up in a cell and, therefore, could have had no hand in the crime. That is to say, that he had no *actual* hand in it, although, as Paul realised, he could quite easily have directed the whole thing, deputing some other person to carry out the actual murder.

Paul frowned as he drove the big car on towards Bromley, and his brother, who was seated at his side, kept a discreet silence. There was something very deep here, of that Paul felt sure. Behind the clouds of doubt and suspicion that obscured his mind, he kept on every now and again getting little flashing glimpses of something that was too intangible to be called a theory.

He pushed his foot on the accelerator to take the slope of Mason's Hill, topped the rise, and slid down towards Prospect Place. He brought the car to a halt at the end of the cul-de-sac where Emily Boulter lived and got out.

'I think you'd better wait here, old chap,' he said to his brother, speaking for the first time since they had left the village of Buckley. 'I shan't be long.'

Bob nodded, and Paul turned into the narrow street and made his way towards the house bearing the worn brass plate.

The string was no longer protruding from the letter-box, and raising his hand he knocked. No deep voice answered him from within the cottage, and he wondered if the gaunt woman was out. It looked very much like it, but he decided to knock again, in case she might be resting and had not heard the first summons. But there was no answer to his second knock either. Nothing but silence. There was nothing for it but to go and have tea somewhere and come back — it was useless leaving a note because he remembered that she had said she couldn't read.

He was in the act of turning to walk down the short path to the gate when he happened to glance at the window and stopped. The spotless curtains that covered it — a tribute to Emily Boulter's laundering — were an inch apart in the centre. Through the gap he could see the shutters that had been closed over the window on the inside. He remembered those shutters. They folded back on each side of the recess in which the window was built. Paul looked closer, and his forehead puckered in a frown. It seemed strange that she should have closed those shutters in the middle of the afternoon; even on that day of rain when he had visited her before, they had been open.

He went nearer, stepping off the little path onto the garden so that he could get quite near to the window, and peered through the glass. And then he uttered a startled exclamation, for the shutters had not only been closed but the joints had been stuffed with paper from the inside.

Paul went back again to the front door,

his face set and a little white. He gripped the handle above the letter-box and shook it. The door was firmly fastened. Next he tried the flap of the letter-box. It had been secured from the inside and was immovable. With rapidly growing alarm, he stepped back two paces and hurled himself at the door. It gave a protesting crack and shivered but held. Twice he flung himself against the barrier, and at the third attempt there was a splintering crash and the door flew back. He almost went with it owing to the force of his rush, but a clutch at the frame saved him from losing his balance.

A great gush of gas-laden air greeted his nostrils and caught chokingly at his throat, and from the dim interior of the room he heard a low monotonous hiss. Pulling out his handkerchief, he clapped it over his nose and mouth, and stumbled across to the point from whence the hissing came. It was the gas-ring in the fireplace on which Emily Boulter heated her irons, and he fumbled for the tap. He found it and turned it off, and the low, malignant hissing ceased.

Groping his way to the door, he gulped in some fresh air, and once more plunged into that gas-charged atmosphere. He found the thing he was seeking — the huddled form of the laundress, her head sunk forward on her chest, seated on a chair beside the table. Seizing the chair, he dragged it and its helpless burden towards the door and into the stream of fresh, life-giving air that was pouring in.

The woman's gaunt face was ominously tinged with blue, but she was still breathing, although Paul realised that it would only have been a question of minutes before she would have succumbed to that poisonous atmosphere.

The open door was rapidly clearing the room of gas, and he calculated that in ten minutes or so it would be safe to venture in. He stood looking out into the small forecourt and waited as patiently as possible. He could do nothing at present for the unconscious Emily Boulter. Her breathing, though faint, was fairly regular, and so was the beating of her heart. The best thing was to let her recover of her own accord, helped by the fresh air which she was now drawing into her lungs. She was, luckily, very healthy, and possessed a remarkable constitution, so that he felt that the after-effects of the gas, though unpleasant, would not prove serious.

In the meanwhile, he wondered just what had happened in this little cottage that afternoon. Was this an attempt at suicide, or something infinitely more sinister? It was really a waste of time to speculate. Emily Boulter, when she recovered, would be able to answer that question finally.

The air of the room was now practically clear. The smell of the gas still hung heavily everywhere, but the air was breathable, and he went inside and looked about him. The interstices of the shutters over the window had been packed with strips of brown paper and handkerchiefs rammed firmly home. The chimney had been closed with several towels — towels that he saw had been freshly washed and ironed, the property without doubt of one of Emily Boulter's customers. He examined the letter-box. Part of an old box lid had been screwed over it behind, and he saw that the screws were fresh ones, their heads new and shiny. Going back into the room, he found on the table a scrap of paper, and picking it up he read the misspelt message scrawled on it in pencil:

'*I done it becos I was lonly.*'

He frowned. From the judgment he had formed of Emily Boulter's character, this was utterly unlike her. Lonely she was, but it was a loneliness of her own seeking and not the kind that would have preyed on her mind and driven her to self-destruction.

Paul stared with narrowed eyes at the paper which he still held in his hand, but he was not looking at it. With the eye of his mind he was looking beyond it, into the realm of conjecture from which had suddenly emerged a startling thought — a thought that was so bizarre that it acted like a splash of cold water. Could it be right? Could this sudden idea that had come to him be the true answer to the problem?

He was still wondering when a sound behind him made him turn quickly, to find that Emily Boulter was recovering from the effects of the gas.

16

Emily Boulter's Story

The first words she uttered were characteristic. 'Help me into the kitchen,' she muttered, 'I'm going to be sick!'

Paul helped her through to the spotless kitchen and tactfully turned his back while the natural results of the gas manifested themselves.

'Now,' she said a few seconds later in a stronger voice, 'if I can have a good strong cup of tea I shall be all right.'

She refused his offer to help, although she was still shaky. Filling the kettle, she brought it into the sitting-room and put it on the gas-ring. While she put the tea in the tea-pot and waited for the kettle to boil, she said nothing, and Paul did not question her, thinking it was best to allow her time to recover. When the tea had been made and she poured out two cups, she began on her own account.

'Sit down, young man,' she said, 'and tell me how you got here and what happened.'

Paul smiled. 'I was hoping you'd be able to tell me what happened.'

'I can tell you up to a point,' she said, sipping her tea with relish. 'But after that it's your turn.'

'Well, let's hear your story first,' he suggested. 'How did all this happen?'

She set down her cup, and her gaunt face was grim. 'It happened because I was a fool!' she said. 'If I'd had any sense, I should have mistrusted the man from the start.'

She went over to the fireplace and turned out the gas under the steaming kettle. Coming back, she sat down by the table, resting her bony elbows on it. Cupping her chin in her hands, she looked steadily at Paul and began her story.

'I never have any food in the middle of the day,' she said. 'A cup of tea and sometimes a slice of bread and butter does me until I've finished my work. I had this today about twelve o'clock, and I'd just finished it when there was a knock on the door. I shouted to whoever it was to pull the string and come in. Well, a man came in. He was a respectable-looking feller but shabbily dressed. His overcoat was shiny and threadbare, but it had been a good one, you could see that; there's no mistaking the cut of a coat. I asked him what he wanted, and he said that he was a plain-clothes police officer, and he had been sent to make further enquiries about what I had told you. I didn't like the look of him at all, and I told him that I'd said all I could say, so what was the good of bothering me anymore.' She paused and took a long drink of tea.

'What happened then?' asked Paul.

'He said that he didn't want to bother me but that it was necessary he should ask me a few questions. And he began to ask me all about the man I'd seen on the bus. I told him what I had told you, and while I was talking I noticed something, and that's why I said just now that I was a fool.'

'What did you notice?' said Paul quietly.

'I noticed his hands,' said Miss Boulter, and her squint became more marked with the intensity of her gaze as she stared at him. 'He'd taken them out of his pockets and was playing with the back of a chair while he talked.' She leaned forward impressively. 'They were the hands of the man I saw on the bus that night — the man who wore the onyx ring.'

'Are you sure of that?' Paul's eyes were shining with suppressed excitement as he put the question to her.

She nodded. 'I'll take me oath on it,' she declared. 'This man didn't look the same. He was fair instead of being white, and wasn't old, but his hands were the same.'

'What did you do?'

'I didn't do anything. It gave me a bit of a shock when I realised that the man I was talking to had killed the old gentleman, but I tried not to let him see I'd noticed anything, while I thought what was best to be done. I think he did notice, though, for I saw him stiffen a bit, and he put his hands back quickly into his pockets. I went on talking about the murder while all the time I was wondering how I could keep the feller until I could get hold of a policeman.

'As it happened, he didn't give me a chance. Suddenly, in the middle of a question, he sprang at me and held a handkerchief over my nose and mouth. It was soaked with something that smelt like rotten apples, and I was so taken by surprise that I couldn't stop him.' She glared at Paul as though he were the man who had done this outrageous thing. 'I put up a fight, though,' she continued grimly. 'But he was a strong customer, and the smell of the stuff on the handkerchief was making me dizzy. I felt a funny, light sensation, and then I don't know what happened. The next thing I remember was waking up and finding myself here.'

'Can you describe the man?' asked Paul.

She frowned. 'He was one of those fellers you wouldn't look at twice in a crowd,' she answered. 'He wasn't tall, and he wasn't short, and his hair and moustache were like yellow straw.'

'Oh, he had a moustache, had he?'

'Yes. One of those ragged affairs that fall over the mouth. I don't know as I'd know him again, except for his hands.'

'What were they like?'

'It isn't easy to tell you in words,' said Emily Boulter, 'but they were funny, rather fat and stubby. I'd know 'em again anywhere.'

'I hope you'll have a chance to identify

them,' said Paul.

'I hope so too,' said the laundress fiercely. 'I'd like to have ten minutes alone with that young man!'

'You've undoubtedly had a very narrow escape,' said Paul gravely. 'His object was murder. He used chloroform to drug you, and then when you were unconscious, sealed up the room, wrote that note to make it look as if you'd committed suicide, turned on the gas, and left — by the back way, presumably.'

'And if you hadn't come along, I should be dead by now,' said the gaunt woman. 'I shan't forget that.' She extended a huge hand and gripped Paul's with a clasp that was like a man's. 'Will you have another cup of tea?' she asked.

He shook his head. 'No, thank you. I really ought to be getting back. My brother is waiting for me in the car, and he'll be wondering where I've got to.'

'Then run along,' said Emily Boulter, much the same as she might have spoken to a small boy. 'I must get on with my work too. Those towels and things will have to be washed again.'

'You're sure you're all right?' said Paul. 'You wouldn't like me to send for a doctor?'

'Good gracious, no! I don't want any doctor messing about me! I've got a bit of a headache, but that's all. If I have a lie down presently, I shall be as right as ninepence.'

Paul was rather reluctant to leave her alone, but she was insistent, and he took his leave. He found Bob waiting rather restlessly.

'Hello!' he greeted as his brother approached the car. 'I was just wondering if I should come and see what had happened. You have been a long time.'

'Couldn't help it, old chap,' said Paul. 'I was nearly chief witness at an inquest.' He got into the car and slid behind the wheel. 'I'll tell you all about it on the way back.'

He did so, to Bob's intense interest. 'What was the object of doing her in?' asked his brother when he had finished.

Paul began to speak rapidly, outlining the amazing idea that had sprung into his mind in Emily Boulter's little sitting-room. He had only just concluded when he brought the car to a halt outside the house at Hampstead.

'What do you think of it?' he asked with a smile as Bob remained silent.

'I think you've hit it,' replied his brother, 'but there are a lot of gaps to fill in, and it's going to take a deuce of a lot of proving.'

'I know it is,' agreed Paul. 'And that's our job from now on.'

17

A Job for Bob

Paul spent the evening quietly, lounging comfortably in his favourite armchair, and smoking with half-closed eyes, only moving to consume the excellent dinner that his cook provided, and returning to his original position immediately after the meal. The more that he thought over the idea that had obtruded on his consciousness like the sudden switching on of a light in a dark room, the more convinced he became that it was the right one. It explained several things that were otherwise unexplainable. At the same time, there still remained a great deal that must be fitted in. But he was certain that he was on the right track, although the bridge between suspicion and certainty was a long one. He went to bed at last, still thinking over the problem, and when at seven-thirty his early morning tea was brought he had come to a definite decision regarding his next move.

Immediately after breakfast he put through a telephone call to Mr. Robin. The inspector had just arrived, and he listened with interest to what his friend had to say, although Paul carefully refrained from mentioning the person on whom his suspicion centred.

'I'll come along in about an hour and a half, Paul,' he promised. 'There are one or two things I've got to see to here first, and then I'll be along.'

The detective hung up the receiver and filled in the time while he was waiting for Mr. Robin's appearance by making notes of his conclusions concerning the Blue Moon mystery. He had barely finished these when the inspector was announced. He looked tired and rather harassed.

'I've been up before the Assistant Commissioner,' he explained when Paul commented on this. 'He wants to know how the case against Lonsdale is going, and seems to think that we've been rather slow. In a nutshell, what he wants is this. We've either got to bring a definite charge against him and get him committed for trial, or release him altogether.'

Paul's face was grave. 'If you release Lonsdale,' he said earnestly, 'you'll be an accessory to murder!'

Round Robin stared at him. 'I don't get you,' he muttered. 'What do you mean?'

'I mean this,' said Paul. 'At the present moment Richard Lonsdale is safe. But once the charge of murder against him is definitely withdrawn, and he is released, his life will be in danger. As I see it, this plot not only involves the murder of William Hooper, but the death of Richard Lonsdale as well to make it successful. If that death is brought about by the law, all well and good, but if it isn't — if the law refuses to hang Lonsdale — then the person at the back of this business will have to take more drastic steps.'

'Who do you think this person is?' asked Mr. Robin quickly.

Paul shook his head. 'I'd rather not say at present,' he said. 'Let's call him Mr. X.'

'Well, I don't see how we can hold Lonsdale much longer,' said Mr. Robin. 'This attempted murder of the woman is a nasty blow to our theory that he's guilty. It would go a long way with a jury, you know, Paul.'

'It certainly would, but if you keep up the fiction of Lonsdale's guilt so far as the public is concerned for a little longer, I think there's a very good chance of our laying our hands on the real murderer.'

'You do, eh?' said Round Robin, and his little twinkling eyes regarded Paul curiously. 'What's the scheme?'

'It's a very simple one,' said Paul, 'but I warn you that it entirely depends on my idea being the right one. If I'm wrong, then it won't work.'

'Well, let's hear it anyway,' grunted Round Robin, dropping into a chair.

'First of all,' answered Paul, 'I'll tell you roughly the conclusions I've reached up to now.' He consulted the notes he had recently made and went on: 'In my opinion, the motive behind the killing of Hooper and the casting of suspicion on Richard Lonsdale is Hooper's money. There's no other motive that would make the removing of Lonsdale a necessity to the plot. Now if we take that as the motive, and for the sake of argument agree that the scheme was to get rid of both Hooper and Lonsdale, the man on whom our suspicions immediately centre is Craven. If Lonsdale is hanged, or dies by any other means, he, as next of kin, automatically comes into two and a half million. Is that clear enough so far?'

Mr. Robin nodded. 'So far,' he agreed. 'And then we come against an insurmountable snag. At the time of the murder, Craven was locked up in a cell at Buckley and couldn't have had anything to do with it.'

'Exactly,' said Paul. 'So for our theory to hold good, we shall have to introduce the person whom I have called X. Supposing X and Craven to be working together, their object being to obtain Hooper's money. They're aware in some way that Lonsdale is Hooper's son, and that Hooper has made a new will in his favour, and they decide to kill Hooper and get Lonsdale hanged for the crime. That gets rid of the two people who are standing in the way of Craven becoming a rich man.

'But Craven and X realise that this scheme might be seen through, and that suspicion might turn to Craven. Therefore, he has got to be provided with an alibi. They hit on the idea of the accident and the assault on the police constable, and so make the police themselves provide him with the essential alibi. No possible suspicion can now attach to Craven whatever happens, and X proceeds to carry out the actual crime, having previously, in his red wig disguise, got hold of the revolver from the Mace's house.

'To complicate matters still further, he wears on the night of the murder a duplicate ring, hoping — I think — that Lonsdale may notice it on the finger of the old man and mention it to the police, who will certainly try and find the passengers on the bus near the time of the crime to get their evidence. The ring will lead indirectly to *Craven*, who can immediately prove that the ring he wears cannot be taken off. The police will at once discredit Lonsdale's statement, and come to the natural conclusion that he was lying about the ring in order to implicate Craven, unaware that the man has a complete alibi. That, roughly, is how I see the affair. What do you think?'

'I think it's a most ingenious and

plausible theory,' said Mr. Robin. 'But it's only a theory, and it's going to take a deuce of a lot of proving. It's next to impossible to connect X with the business.'

'That's where the whole thing has been worked out so cleverly,' said Paul. 'There is not the slightest doubt that if Lonsdale is hanged for this crime, the money would be passed to Craven without demur, and nobody could stop it.'

'Unless in the meantime Lonsdale made another will,' said Mr. Robin. 'That would stop it.'

'Yes, that would stop it,' assented the detective. 'But in the ordinary course of events, Craven would get the money and could divide it up with his confederate.'

'And you say you know who this fellow you call X is?' demanded Round Robin.

'No,' answered Paul. 'I said I *think* I know who he is, but my suspicion is based on such a slender fact that I don't feel justified in revealing it.'

'But you've got some kind of a scheme for making certain,' said Mr. Robin. 'What is it?'

'It's this,' said Paul. 'If my idea is correct

— my theory of the whole plot, I mean — then Craven, once he's free, will almost certainly, sooner or later, try and get in touch with X. I suggest that Bob should keep a close watch on him and find out who he sees, and that you should arrange that all his letters and telephone calls are supervised.'

'That's a good idea,' said the inspector, nodding approvingly. 'I can arrange that. The feller comes up before the magistrate today. I'll arrange that he's let off with a caution and a fine.'

They discussed the plan in further detail, and then Mr. Robin took his leave. Bob was delighted when he heard that at last he was going to take an active part in finding the murderer of William Hooper — a delight that might have been tempered with apprehension could he have looked into the future, for his shadowing of Leslie Craven was to very nearly cost him his life.

18

The Club in Soho

Leslie Craven was severely censured by a stern-faced magistrate, fined £20 and costs, and had his driving licence suspended for two years. He bowed to the magistrate, paid his fine, and, leaving the court, went straight to the railway station, where he took a ticket to London.

Bob Rivington travelled on the same train, and when Craven let himself into a small flat in Gerrard Street, he was close on his heels. For three days, he and a man called Birch — an ex-detective whom Paul occasionally engaged for such purposes — kept a close watch on Craven's movements, working in day and night shifts, without discovering anything to reward their diligence. He seldom went out except for a walk, during which he neither met nor spoke to a single soul. Mr. Robin reported that no letters or telephone calls

135

had been sent or received by him, and the thing seemed to be developing into a dead end. Bob was getting thoroughly bored and fed up, and had come to the conclusion that his watch was nothing more than a waste of time, when on the fourth night something did happen to make the prospect look a little brighter.

It was his turn for night duty. Birch had been at his post all day, and when Bob relieved him at ten o'clock he reported that nothing had occurred at all. Craven had not even left his flat for his usual walk, but had remained in all day and was there still.

'And it looks to me as if he were going to remain there all night,' said Birch. 'He never comes out again as late as this.'

'Thoroughly cheerful, aren't you?' growled Bob, and the big man grinned. 'Well, go along to your supper and your nice warm bed, and if it comes on to snow in the night, just tuck yourself up a little warmer and think of me!'

He settled himself down to his vigil, a not very desirable task, for though he had exaggerated about the snow, the night was certainly a cold one. A chill wind had sprung up and there was a hint of rain in the air.

Bob huddled in his overcoat, then walked to the end of the street and back again. He could do this without losing sight of the doorway he was watching, and it helped to break the deadly monotony. By now he knew every stick and stone of Gerrard Street, and was getting heartily sick of the sight of it.

He paused at the corner of a side turning and gazed up at the lights of Shaftesbury Avenue. That thoroughfare was partly deserted, but in another half hour would be teeming with people and traffic when the theatres disgorged their audiences. He had seen it happen before; one moment quiet, and the next, filled with taxis and buses and pedestrians tumbling over each other and scrambling in their mad rush to get home or on to the restaurants where they were taking supper. Tonight he saw it again, and saw it gradually sink back to quiet as the rush dwindled. Then, to add to the unpleasantness of his task, it began to rain. It started as a drizzle, but by twelve o'clock it was a downpour.

He took refuge in a doorway and watched the drops dancing in the gutter. This was a part of his work that he heartily disliked — this hanging about waiting for something that never happened — and yet it was a very important part. In order to while away the time, he began to count the number of similar expeditions on which he had been engaged, and he was in the midst of this when he was startled into sudden alertness by seeing somebody leave the shadow of the house he was watching. At first he scarcely hoped it could be Craven; and then the man, walking hurriedly up the street, passed under a light standard, and Bob saw that it was.

Something was moving at last. This was the most promising thing that had happened so far, for the time was well after one, and on such a night it must have been something urgent to have brought the man out.

Bob followed at a discreet distance, wondering where the man was making for. He was soon to know, for crossing Shaftesbury Avenue, Craven plunged into the maze of streets on the opposite side known as Soho. At a narrow door in a mean turning he stopped, and after a quick glance round, entered the dimly lighted vestibule.

Bob glanced at the broken sign hanging above and whistled softly. Maroc's! One of the smallest and shadiest of the remaining nightclubs. A place in which the lowest of London's underworld congregated nightly, and allowed to remain open only because it was useful to the police. Bob knew Maroc, the polyglot owner — a fat, greasy man. What had brought Leslie Craven to this place?

Bob frowned, and sauntering slowly along on the opposite side of the street, considered what he should do next. He could, of course, wait until Craven came out, but in that case the man would in all probability merely go home, and he would learn nothing. If there was anything happening, it was happening inside the dingy club. It was more than likely that the very thing Paul had anticipated was now taking place, and that Craven had come to keep an appointment with the mysterious X, the killer of William Hooper.

If that was the case, it was essential that he — Bob — should see who the man was, and in order to do this he would have, by some means or other, to get inside Maroc's. But it was much easier to decide this than to do it. He was not a member, and Maroc's was not the kind of place that would welcome strangers.

He stopped at the corner of the street, from which point he could still see the entrance to the place, and thought hard. Several schemes suggested themselves, but he rejected them all. How could he get into the confounded place without arousing suspicion?

At the expiration of fifteen minutes he began to feel a little irritable. Here was a heaven-sent chance for discovering something vital, and he couldn't take advantage of it. It was enough to make anybody annoyed, particularly after the hours he had put in watching Craven without result. He saw several people come along and pass into the dingy-looking entrance while he waited, and ground his teeth.

There must be some way, surely. And then like a flash it came to him. If only the man he wanted was there, it would be a complete solution to his problem, and it was an even chance that he would be. Anyway, it was worth trying. The first thing he would have to find was a telephone. The nearest call-box that would be usable at that hour was in Leicester Square, and it would take him a few minutes to get to it, put through his call and get back. In the meanwhile, Craven and the man he had gone to meet — if he had gone to meet anyone at all — might quite easily leave Maroc's. Bob decided that he would have to risk that, and set off as quickly as he could for the call-box. It was easy enough to find Maroc's number, and presently he heard a smooth, rather oily voice come over the wire.

'Is Mr. Crick there?' he asked, and the voice replied that if he would give his name an enquiry would be made.

'This is the *News-Bulletin* speaking,' said Bob. 'It's rather urgent.'

The oily voice asked him to hold on, and Bob waited. He heard over the wire a confused murmur of voices and the tinny strains of a dance band, and then a different voice from the firm suddenly said: 'Hello!'

'Hello!' said Bob. 'Is that you, Crick? Listen, this is Bob Rivington speaking. I gave the *News-Bulletin* because I didn't want to give my own name. I want to see you for a minute, old man. Can you come out and meet me just outside the club in five minutes' time? No, I can't explain over the phone. Will you? Thanks so much. Yes, five minutes.'

He hung up the receiver and left the call-box. So far so good. It only remained now for him to persuade Crick to take him into Maroc's, and all would be plain sailing. He hurried back as fast as he could to the place of his appointment.

It had been a brainwave to think of Crick. He was a journalist who specialised in the night life of London, and was a habitué of most of the haunts that are wakeful when the greater part of the metropolis is sleeping. Bob had met him on several occasions, for he was a close friend of Paul Rivington's, and often dropped into the house at Hampstead for a smoke and a chat.

He saw a little man at the door of Maroc's as he turned into the street, and gave a soft whistle. Crick looked keenly in his direction and then came towards him.

'What's the game?' he asked as he shook hands. 'Why have you dragged me out of my den of iniquity into the cold of this miserable night?'

Bob told him as briefly as possible, and when he had finished Crick pursed his lips. 'You promise you won't make any trouble at Maroc's?' he asked anxiously. 'Because I wouldn't like anything like that to happen through me. They treat me very decently at these places, and I'm sort of on my honour not to do anything that might get them into trouble. I can take you in all right — they won't question anybody that I sponsor, and for that reason I wouldn't let them down.'

'I won't make any trouble, Crick,' said Bob. 'I only want to see if this fellow Craven meets anyone.'

'He hasn't met anyone yet,' said the journalist, 'and I've never seen him before in my life. He's certainly not a habitual haunter of night clubs, or I should have done. However, he must know somebody who's a member, or he wouldn't have been able to get in. Maroc's is very strict about that.'

'Well, will you take me in?' asked Bob.

The other hesitated for a moment and then nodded. 'Yes, I'll take you in. Come along.'

He led the way back along a narrow street, and together they passed through the doorway. A man in a rather shabby lounge suit was seated behind a small counter at one side of the entrance, and Crick went over to him and whispered something. The man — an unprepossessing individual who looked like a retired boxer — glanced sharply over at Bob and nodded, pushing a greasy-looking book towards the journalist. Crick took the pencil that was tied to it with string, scribbled something in the book, and came over to his waiting companion.

'Come along,' he said, and, pushing open a door that faced them, shepherded Bob into a narrow passage that appeared to run through to the back. It was lit by a hanging lamp covered with a shade of pink silk rather the worse for wear, which shed a subdued light over everything. Halfway down, the passage widened, and along one side had been fixed a narrow counter, behind which were rows of pegs supporting a collection of coats and hats.

Bob left his coat with the man in charge of this extempore cloakroom and received a check in exchange. He could hear the sound of a band close at hand, and then as Joseph Crick opened a pair of folding doors, the full blare of a foxtrot burst upon his ears. A blaze of light greeted him, and he found himself standing on top of a flight of three steps, gazing down onto the dance floor of Maroc's.

19

The Crippled Man

Maroc's was, before it was taken over by its present proprietor and put to baser uses, a mission hall; a large, bare, barn-like place, the roof of which was supported on iron girders that crossed from wall to wall. Maroc had had the place garishly painted with pictures of desert scenes and languorous lagoons, but the original building peeped through this faded splendour like the bones in an X-ray photograph. The floor had been covered with a layer of sprung parquet, on which the shoes of the habitués nightly shuffled to the strains of a raucous orchestra that stirred the jaded senses of the bored dancers.

Around this small rectangle of polished wood were set two score or more of little scarlet tables, each with its complement of scarlet-painted wicker chairs, and at these sat a heterogeneous collection of humanity drawn from all parts of the globe. Painted women languidly walked back and forth in the arms of their partners to the time of the row dinned out ceaselessly by the band on the raised dais at the end of the room.

The atmosphere was heavy with tobacco smoke and the sickly smell of cheap perfume. There was something terribly sad about the tired-eyed women, whose lips were curled in a perpetual, mechanical, mirthless smile, and the hard, bored faces of the men. They were all trying so desperately to enjoy themselves. That was the impression that came to Bob Rivington. The wailing of the band, the shuffling 'swish, swish' of the dancers' feet, and the noisy laughter were an attempt to drown the thoughts that might otherwise crowd into the brains of these derelicts of humanity and prove even less pleasant than this hectic, spurious excitement. They dare not stop; they must go on doing something, anything, until they were so tired physically and mentally or had so dulled their senses with drink that they could creep away to their neglected beds and sleep — and sleeping, forget themselves and life, and what they had made of it.

Crick caught the expression on his face and grimaced. 'Nice crew, aren't they?' he whispered as he took Bob's arm and led him down the steps and round the edges of the dance floor. 'You'll find the same lot here night after night doing exactly the same thing. When the dawn breaks they slink away to their holes and stop there until it's dark again. It's probably such a long time since the majority have seen the sun that they've forgotten it exists.' He sat down at a table, and with the toe of his shoe jerked forward a chair.

'What a life,' muttered Bob as he sat down opposite his companion.

'It's of their own choosing,' said the journalist, shrugging his shoulders. 'Most of 'em wouldn't understand any other. I've spoken to 'em and I know.'

He beckoned to a pallid-faced waiter and gave an order while Bob glanced about in search of Leslie Craven. He saw him seated at a table to their left, staring rather contemptuously at the crowded dance floor. A half-finished whisky stood before him, and the light glistened on the setting of the onyx ring. As Bob watched him he glanced over towards the entrance, and his hand resting on the table moved impatiently. Was he expecting someone? That quick look at the door and the ceaseless movement that had accompanied it rather suggested that he was. Bob sincerely hoped so, anyway.

He only allowed his eyes to rest on Craven casually, and then his glance passed on. It stopped at the stout evening-dress-clad figure of Maroc standing, a cigar in the corner of his thick-lipped mouth, by the side of the band platform. He was talking to a woman in a vivid green dress, and from her expression the conversation was anything but a pleasant one. Twice she shook her head, and then her overly red lips quivered as though she were going to cry. Maroc took his cigar out of his mouth with a sudden movement, and the expression on his face was ugly as he snarled something at her, accompanying his remark, whatever it was, with a peremptory movement of his fat, none-too-clean hand.

The woman — she was, so Bob judged, still in her early twenties — looked at him as though she were going to protest, and then without a word she moved away and disappeared through a curtained recess at the side of the orchestra dais. Maroc, without a glance in her direction, began to cross the tiny dance floor, threading his way among the couples. Reaching the other side of the room, he sat down at a table occupied by a man nearly twice as fat as himself, and the pair began an earnest conversation.

Bob watched this piece of by-play and wondered what it was all about. The woman who had disappeared through the curtained archway was being forced to do something that she did not want to do, that was obvious, and the something was connected with the foreign-looking man to whom Maroc was now speaking, for he looked over his shoulder at the place where the woman had gone.

'Who is that fellow?' he asked.

Crick smiled. 'That fellow is Veetshein,' answered the journalist. 'He owns a string of dance halls abroad.'

'And the woman?' asked Bob. 'The woman in green who Maroc was talking to?'

Crick shook his head. 'I don't know. I've never seen her before. She came in just before you telephoned, and that's the first time I've ever set eyes on her.'

Bob opened his mouth to say something more, and stopped as his attention was attracted by a newcomer. The door at the top of the three steps had opened, and a man had appeared, a man with jet-black hair that fell lankly over his forehead and threw into vivid relief his almost dead-white face. And what a face! The lips were thin, and the scar than ran up one side of his cheek had by its contraction pulled up one side of his mouth so that he appeared to be eternally smiling; a sneering smile that found no counterpart in his eyes. He was dressed in an ill-fitting dinner suit, and standing on the steps he shot a quick, searching glance round the whole place. His eyes — the lids of which remained half-closed — rested for a fraction of a second on the table occupied by Leslie Craven, and Bob saw that Craven had seen and recognised the newcomer.

So this was the man he had been waiting for!

Bob felt his pulse beating faster. Was this man the passenger on the Blue Moon — White-wig, the murderer of William Hooper? He was not the least like the description Paul had given him of the man, but he had been disguised then, and there was no reason why he should not be disguised now.

Bob watched him as he descended the three steps and began to cross the floor towards Craven. The band had just finished playing a foxtrot, and in spite of the applause appeared to have decided to have a short rest. The dance floor began to clear as the couples drifted towards their respective tables, and as a result, Bob was able to get a good view of the man. He noticed that he walked with a pronounced limp, dragging his left foot behind him as though the leg were partially paralysed. This might be part and parcel of the disguise. If it were not, then this unpleasant-looking newcomer could not be the man of the bus, because he had not been crippled. Bob saw the limping man come up to Craven's table and sit down. Craven looked rather annoyed, and it seemed to Bob that his annoyance was due to being kept waiting, for he glanced at the watch on his wrist and made some remark to which the other replied with a long explanation.

Bob turned towards his companion and found that Crick was watching him interestedly. 'Who's that fellow who's just come in?' he asked.

'They call him Marlowe,' answered the journalist. 'But whether that's his real name or not, I wouldn't like to say. He's been here once or twice before, but he doesn't come often. Who he is, or what he is, I don't know.'

Bob took a sip of the drink which had stood neglected in front of him, and once more gave a casual glance towards Craven's table. The crippled man and his companion were deep in conversation, with their heads close together. He would have given a great deal to have heard what they were discussing, but that was impossible. However, things had progressed much better than he had anticipated or expected. He had been beginning to think, after three days without result of any kind, that Paul had been wrong in his theory, but now it looked as if his brother was right. Certainly something was afoot, and if it had nothing to do with the killing of William Hooper it would be a very strange coincidence.

Bob came to the conclusion that his best course would be to keep an eye on the limping man when he left. Craven wasn't important. They knew where to find him when they wanted him, but this other man was — if Paul was right — the key to the whole problem, and it was essential to find out all about him. He settled himself comfortably to wait until the man he was interested in should show signs of departure. And he had a long wait, for it was nearly two hours before his quarry showed a disposition to move.

By this time the club was beginning to empty. By ones and twos and in little parties, the habitués began to drift towards the exit and disappear. Most of them, Crick informed him, would be going on to the Caterpillar, a new club that had recently been opened in Tottenham Court Road.

'It'll be raided and shut within a fortnight,' said the journalist, 'but just at present it's a novelty. Why the police haven't closed this place before is a mystery to me.'

It was no mystery to Bob. He had once discussed the night-club question with Mr. Robin, and the Scotland Yard man had told him that a few of these places were allowed to keep going because they were useful. A certain class of criminal frequents them regularly, and they act as a sort of concentration point. Besides which, a great deal of useful information can be picked up from the people who run them.

'In return for being allowed to break the law and sell drinks after hours,' the cherubic inspector had said, 'they're willing to act as 'noses'. That fellow Maroc, for instance, has more than once been able to give us valuable information. If he didn't spill the beans when we want him to, we should close him up in a week, and he knows it.'

Bob was in the middle of explaining this to Crick when out of the corner of his eye he saw the limping man rise to his feet and say goodnight to Craven.

Instantly he gave a signal to Crick, and the journalist proceeded to do what they had previously arranged. He got up, yawned, and in a fairly loud voice remarked: 'Well, I think I'll be getting along. What about you?'

'I'm ready,' said Bob. 'Let's go.'

Without even glancing in the direction

of his quarry, he followed Crick across to the steps and out to the cloakroom. As they were collecting their coats and hats, he saw the cripple come along and hand in his check. Still chatting to Crick about nothing in particular, Bob struggled into his overcoat and, linking his arm in that of his friend, passed out of the club.

A taxi came swinging round the corner out of the Haymarket, and the crippled man hailed it, gave a quick direction to the driver, and getting in, slammed the door. The taxi turned and began to run along Coventry Street, gathering speed. Bob, his heart sinking at the possibility of losing his quarry after all, looked round for another, and luckily saw one just emerging from Regent Street. The driver drew up beside him at his signal, and Bob pulled open the door.

'Follow that cab,' he said quickly, pointing towards the rear light of the taxi containing the crippled man, and jumped inside.

20

The House at Dulwich

Bob settled himself back in the cab and prepared for what was destined to be a long chase. The taxi in front sped down Whitehall, passed over Westminster Bridge and along Westminster Bridge Road into Kennington, swung round at the Oval, and went on towards Camberwell Green. He began to wonder how much further they were going. Certainly the crippled man had come a long enough distance to keep his appointment with Craven.

On they went, the road ahead getting momentarily lighter as the dawn came. The grey of early morning began to give place to a warmer hue as the sky became tinged with the light of the rising sun. They had left the main road now and were negotiating a maze of narrow side streets until Bob became completely lost as to their whereabouts.

The first inkling he had of their locality

was when they suddenly emerged from the network of side turnings and came out onto a broad thoroughfare that seemed familiar. Peering out through the side window, he caught a glimpse of a name plate high up on the wall of a house: 'London Road'.

He looked ahead at the steep hill and saw part of a square tower with a clock in it rising out of a screen of trees, and recognising the landmark, he realised where he was. The tower was the tower of Horniman's Museum, and they were, therefore, at Forest Hill. If they continued in the direction in which they were travelling, they would shortly be at Dulwich. But apparently they had reached the end of the journey, for as the cab in front passed the museum on the top of the hill and began to run down the other side, it slowed and drew in towards the kerb.

Bob leaned forward and tapped on the window to attract the attention of his own driver, and hastily letting it down, leaned out. 'Turn round this next side street and stop,' he ordered, and the taxi man nodded, swung his cab sharply to the right and pulled up.

Bob jumped out almost before it had come to a halt and, taking some money from his pocket, thrust it into the man's willing palm. 'Keep the change, and thanks,' he said hastily, and hurried back to the corner of the street. He was just in time to see the crippled man limping away from his taxi, which was in the act of moving off. Bob prepared to follow him.

He continued along the main road until he had passed the fire station, which stood on the left at the bottom of the hill, and then turned into a winding road lined on either side with rather attractive, low-built houses. It seemed to Bob to be rather a prosperous neighbourhood, and he wondered if the man he was following lived here.

Apparently he did not, for he never stopped, but hurried on with his peculiar rapid shuffle that enabled him to move at an amazing rate. Right through the small streets of Dulwich Village he went, and on to a newly made road that was still in the process of construction. Only two houses were finished, the rest consisting of half-brick walls and unpainted wood in a forest of scaffold poles and planks. The whole spot looked very desolate and miserable, for it was too early yet for the workmen engaged on the construction of these 'desirable residences' to have put in an appearance.

Halfway along the road, the crippled man turned off and began to strike across a field. He glanced sharply behind him as he did so, and Bob had only just time to hide himself behind a heap of sacks and escape being seen.

His quarry was making for a gate in a high hedge that bordered the other side of the field, and Bob decided that he would have to wait until he reached it before he came out from his place of concealment. The field offered no cover at all, and it was too risky to attempt to follow him until he was out of sight, for if he took it into his head to look back, nothing could prevent him becoming aware of his trailer's presence.

Bob, therefore, remained where he was and watched the figure of the limping man growing smaller and smaller as he neared his objective. Presently he reached the gate, opened it and, passing through, disappeared from view behind the screening hedge.

Bob waited for a moment or so, and then he too set off towards the gate. Although he hurried as fast as he could, the field was bigger than it looked, and by the time he reached the gate and found himself in the lane that ran along the other side, there was no sign of his quarry. He had made a note of the fact that he had turned to the left when he had passed the gate, however, and set off in this direction.

The lane was very narrow, little more than a cattle track, and turned and twisted to such a degree that it was impossible to see more than a few yards ahead. A little way along it began to widen, and presently broadened out into quite a respectable road. This remained fairly straight, and Bob looked ahead in the hope of sighting the man he was following, but there was no sign of him.

He had walked twenty yards or so when he came upon a small gate. It was set in the bordering hedge and was almost invisible until he was almost on top of it. He paused and looked at it. Could the crippled man have gone through? It would account for his not being anywhere in sight, and the gate looked as though it might lead to a house.

He hesitated for a second or two and then, making up his mind, he glanced quickly about him to make sure that he was not overlooked, opened the gate and slipped through. There was a narrow overgrown path on the other side that wound its way among a small forest of thickly growing trees, and along this he cautiously made his way.

The path took a sharp bend round a clump of evergreen, and he saw before him a rather dilapidated cottage. It was small and in a very bad state of repair, but apparently it was inhabited, for there were curtains at the windows, and one of the upper sashes was half-open. He stopped in the shadow of the shrubbery and considered what he should do next. If this was where the crippled man had gone, then all he had to do was to make a note of the place and go back to Hampstead and report to his brother — but he could not be certain. How was he to get that knowledge?

He was in the act of looking round for a suitable point of vantage — a point from which he could see the cottage without himself being seen — when a faint rustling behind him made him swing round.

At the same instant something crashed down on his head — a violent blow that sent him reeling backwards. He had a momentary glimpse of a white, distorted face close to his own, and then pain and darkness blotted out everything like the switching out of an electric light!

21

Paul Gets Anxious

Paul Rivington came down to breakfast on the morning of Bob's excursion to Dulwich in pursuit of the crippled man, to find a bulky letter among his correspondence. The postmark bore the Victoria district imprint, and as he saw this his interest increased. Ripping it open, he withdrew a number of closely typewritten sheets, and with them a short covering letter.

'Dear Rivington,' it ran, 'here is all the information I can get you regarding the matter we spoke about. I hope it proves of service. Drop in again soon for a chat.
'Sincerely,
'DAVID MARLE.'

Paul laid the letter aside and, spreading the typed sheets beside his plate, began to read them while he ate his breakfast. There was a more detailed account of the robbery of the Southern Bank of Canada than had appeared in his cutting, and it seemed that the Canadian police had made every effort to trace Lonsdale and Warne and the money, but without success. They had, however, succeeded in tracing Warne as far as California, where they had lost him. Mrs. Craven and her son had apparently disappeared from the house where they had been living almost directly after the execution of her husband, and had not appeared again until five years afterwards when she had been located in New York. She was, however, now the wife of William Hooper, one of the new millionaires who had suddenly burst upon Wall Street with a series of startling speculations.

The marriage had been a secret one, but an inquisitive newspaper man had ferreted it out and also discovered that she was the widow of the Southern Bank murderer. The yellow press had seized upon this with glee, with the result that Mrs. Hooper had been visited by the police and subjected to a vigorous cross-examination concerning the reason for her sudden disappearance, where she had gone, and what she knew about Lonsdale and Warne. She said she knew nothing of either, but that after the trial of her husband and his subsequent execution she had felt the disgrace so keenly that she decided to go away with her son to a place where she was unknown. She had gone to a little village in Alberta, and here, while he was on a holiday, she had met William Hooper.

Leslie Craven, her son, bore out these statements, and the police, if not satisfied, had to be content. A year after, a son was born to the Hoopers, and when the child had reached the age of two a fresh sensation was provided in the newspapers. While out with his nurse in Central Park, the boy was kidnapped. William Hooper and his wife were heartbroken, and everything that could be done to find the boy was done.

Hooper offered a reward of twenty thousand dollars, and the police hunted high and low, but the child had vanished completely and there was no trace of him. The nurse could not help at all. A man had come up to her while she was playing with the boy and asked her the time, and then suddenly and without warning clapped a handkerchief soaked with chloroform over her face and held it there until she had lost consciousness.

The police had been rather inclined to suspect the stepson, Leslie Craven, at first, for there was no doubt that the arrival of a son to the Hoopers had jeopardised his prospects, and he was known to be rather a wild youth; but they could not prove anything. At the time of the kidnapping he was at home with his mother, and this alibi could not be shaken.

During the years that followed, William Hooper had never once given up his search for the boy. The famous firm of Pinkertons was engaged to try and find him, but without any success. Why he had been kidnapped at all was not discovered, but it certainly wasn't for money, for Hooper doubled and redoubled the reward without the slightest effect.

This was the gist of the reports that Marie had sent Paul, and he read them with a slight frown. What had happened to Warne? Nobody seemed to know. He had completely vanished with Lonsdale after the robbery, but unlike Lonsdale, there had been no further trace of him. Unless ... He stopped suddenly in his pacing of the room and his eyes narrowed as a possible suggestion presented itself. Supposing Hooper had been Warne!

Quickly he ran over the facts as he knew them. There was nothing against the idea, but what did it lead to? Going quickly over to his desk, he picked up a pencil and drew a sheet of paper towards him. As he pieced together this fresh idea in his mind, he noted it down, and when he had finished he had compiled the following interesting document:

Lonsdale and Warne get away after the robbery of the Southern Bank of Canada, taking the money with them, and allowing Craven to take the rap for the policeman's death. They probably split up, since they would know that a hue and cry would be out after them and that together they would stand more chance of being caught. Warne takes the money and, adopting the name of Hooper, makes a getaway. He joins Mrs. Craven in Alberta and lies low until the excitement following the robbery and the execution of Craven dies down.

Lonsdale, in the meantime, has lost sight of him — probably Warne had promised to communicate with his confederate — and when the time passes and Lonsdale receives no word, he comes to the conclusion that Warne has double-crossed him.

This is exactly what Warne has done, and with the proceeds of the robbery lays the foundation for his future enormous wealth, and sinks his identity in the personality of William Hooper, the millionaire. He eventually marries Mrs. Craven and goes to New York. Lonsdale, in the meanwhile, consumed with rage against the perfidy of the man he trusted, sets out to find him. He succeeds and plans to abduct the boy Richard to revenge himself, knowing that Hooper is passionately fond of his son.

Paul laid down his pencil and read through his notes with satisfaction. This was not only a plausible theory, but he felt sure that it was the right one. It fitted the facts so exactly and cleared up all the ragged threads. That part of the problem which preceded the murder on the Blue Moon was now clear, provided that this was the truth. Hooper, eventually despairing of finding his missing son, had made a will leaving his property to Leslie Craven after the death of his wife — probably at her wish. And then had come news. One or other of the enquiry agents whom he had engaged must have succeeded in tracing the missing boy to Richard Lonsdale, and Hooper had come to England to meet his death at the hands of — whom?

Paul glanced at his watch and saw that it was half past ten. Bob ought to have been back by now, for Birch was due to relieve him at nine. Had something occurred at last? Paul settled himself down to attend to the rest of his morning mail, and this occupied him until twelve, but still there was no sign of his brother. He decided to go round to Gerrard Street and see if he could see anything of Birch. Perhaps Bob had gone off somewhere. He put on his hat and coat, and leaving word that he would be in for lunch, set off.

He found Birch strolling along on the opposite side of the street to Craven's flat, and the man, as he recognised him, increased his pace and came quickly towards him.

'Good morning, Birch,' greeted Paul. 'What's happened to Mr. Robert?'

'That's what's been worrying me, sir,'

said the ex-policeman with a worried frown. 'Haven't you seen him?'

Paul shook his head. 'No. Wasn't he here when you came to relieve him?'

'No, he wasn't. I haven't seen him since last night.'

'Perhaps he's following Craven,' suggested Paul.

'No, he isn't, sir,' answered Birch quickly. 'Craven came out and bought a paper a few minutes ago and went back again. He's still in his flat.'

Paul pursed his lips. 'Well, he must have struck something,' he said. 'Probably I shall hear from him before the day's out.'

He stayed and chatted to the man for a few minutes and then went back to Hampstead. Lunchtime came and went, and Paul sat down with a book, for in case Bob should ring up he wanted to be on the spot. But the afternoon faded into evening, and there was no call from his brother.

At nine o'clock the front door bell rang and he heard the maid cross the hall to answer it, and immediately afterwards a voice that he knew enquired if he was in. There came a man's footsteps, and presently the maid ushered into the room Joseph Crick.

'Hello, Rivington,' greeted the journalist. 'You look very cosy. Hope I'm not disturbing you?'

'I'm very glad to see you,' said Paul. 'Make yourself at home. You'll find cigars and whisky on that table. Help yourself.'

Crick did so, and came back to a chair opposite Paul, carrying a sizzling glass and a cigar. 'I saw your brother last night,' he said after they had exchanged a few remarks about nothing in particular.

Paul looked across at him quickly. 'Did you? Where?'

'In Maroc's,' answered the journalist, and he related exactly what had happened.

'What time was it when he left you to follow this crippled man?' asked Paul when he had finished.

Crick thought for a moment. 'Somewhere about half-past four,' he answered.

Paul looked at the clock. The hands pointed to just ten minutes to ten. Nearly eighteen hours had elapsed since Bob had left the journalist outside Maroc's club.

'I don't like it,' he said gravely. 'I don't like it at all.'

22

Bob's Ordeal

Hammers pounding violently with a dull roar of machinery; a hissing of steam and the rush of many waters ...

Bob stirred uneasily, and a faint groan escaped from between his clenched teeth. He opened his eyes and stared up at a blackened and broken expanse of plaster. His head felt as though it was lying in boiling water, but he discovered that the sounds that he had mistaken for machinery and pounding hammers were inside his brain and not external to himself as he had at first supposed.

The mists were clearing now, and he saw that the cracked and blackened plaster at which he was staring was a ceiling. Dropping his eyes without moving his head, he could make out part of a wall with faded flowery paper, grimy, and in places torn. Presently when the pain in his head had subsided a little, he was able to see more of his surroundings.

He was lying on an old horse-hair-covered sofa in a shabbily furnished room that was long and narrow and rather dusty. There was one latticed window that admitted a modicum of light, and opposite this a fairly solid-looking door. The floor was covered by a carpet that at one time had probably boasted some part of a pattern, but was now a uniform drab colour. The whole place exhaled an atmosphere of sordidness that was most depressing.

He found that he had not been gagged, and came to the conclusion that since this had been omitted, shouting would help him very little. When he had recovered from the dizziness that had attacked him on first coming to his senses, and when the pain in his head had abated to some extent, he tried to see if there was any chance of loosening his bonds, but he quickly discovered that his captor had made a very good job of securing him. He was trussed up like a fowl, and the cords had been drawn so tightly that any slight give in their tension made no appreciable difference.

Allowing his muscles to relax, he lay back and, staring up at the ceiling, set himself to evolve some method by which he could escape. Every possible and impossible suggestion passed through his brain, but none of them were practical. The house was still both inside and out, and he came to the conclusion that the crippled man was either sleeping or had left. He had no idea of the time, for owing to his hands having been tied behind his back, he couldn't see his watch.

It was still daylight outside, but whether it was morning or afternoon he had no way of telling. Presently, while he was still thinking, he dropped into a doze, and he must have slept for a considerable time because when he awoke the room was in partial darkness and the light from the window had faded to a greyish-blue. So the evening was coming on, was it? This first conscious thought was immediately followed by an acute sensation of extreme hunger.

The blue-grey light at the window faded to blackness, and he lay in the dark, his hunger and thirst increasing with every minute. And then when it seemed that the night was far advanced, he heard a sound — the sound of a footfall on the path outside. With straining ears he listened. The footsteps came nearer, and now he was able to distinguish the dragging slur of the crippled leg. His captor was coming back!

From somewhere that sounded very far away, he heard the click of a key, and then the soft thudding of a closing door. This was followed by the complete cessation of all sound — a sudden dead hush. It seemed to him, listening in the darkness, that an age passed before he again heard the shuffling steps, this time on bare boards, and approaching the room in which he lay.

They came nearer and stopped; there was the rasping of a drawn bolt and the snap of a lock spring, and the darkness was dispersed by the dim yellow flame of a candle. Behind this flickering light, Bob could make out the shadowy form of the crippled man. The light caught his dead-white face and made it stand out from the shadows with rather a startling effect.

For a moment the newcomer stood on the threshold, and Bob could see his eyes peering forward in the direction of the couch. It was only for a moment that he remained there, and then, shielding the candle-flame with his hand, he advanced towards the table and set the candle down.

He was no longer dressed in the evening suit in which he had appeared at Maroc's, but was wearing an ill-fitting lounge suit of some dark material. His whole appearance, accentuated by the dragging foot, was indescribably sinister. There was something evil and unclean about it. Leaving the candle burning on the table, he came over to the couch and looked down at his prisoner.

'Well,' he said in a thin cracked treble, 'how are you feeling now?'

Bob met his gaze coolly. 'No better for seeing you,' he retorted briefly.

The crippled man gave a little shrill chuckle. 'I should like to take you in hand,' he remarked. 'You're too fresh! You were remarkably foolish to have followed me last night. I recognised you directly you came into Maroc's, and I guessed that you would follow me when I left. It was rather amusing.' He chuckled again.

'I'm glad you enjoyed it,' said Bob tersely.

'Oh, I did. I can assure you that I haven't

been so amused for a long time.'

'You'll no doubt be a great deal more amused before long,' remarked Bob pleasantly. 'You'll smile at the trial, and I expect when they hang you you'll laugh yourself to death!'

The face above him changed. The thin lips curled back in a snarl, showing, to Bob's surprise, a set of remarkably white and even teeth. 'They'll never hang me,' said the crippled man softly. 'They aren't clever enough. I've got more brains than all of them put together.'

'Every crook thinks that,' said Bob. 'They're all eaten up with a colossal vanity.'

'You cannot class me with the ordinary crook,' retorted the other. 'I agree with you that they're mostly fools, but I'm different.'

'They all think they're different,' said Bob. 'But the only difference about them is the length of their sentences.'

'I shall get no sentence, because I shall never be caught,' said the crippled man with conviction. 'I have guarded against every eventuality.' He nodded several times with great satisfaction. 'I've taken the utmost precautions to cover my tracks. You are the only person I have to fear, and I can assure you that you won't be able to do me any harm.'

'What are you going to do with me?' asked Bob steadily.

'I'm going to kill you,' answered the other calmly, and without emotion. 'There is no other way. That's why I've come back here.' He waited, evidently expecting an answer, but receiving none he went on: 'I'll tell you exactly how you'll die. I've given the matter a great deal of thought, and I don't want your body to be found. I want you just to disappear without a trace, and I've found a way in which it can be done.'

He paused again, but still Bob remained silent.

'This house has a very convenient cellar,' he continued. 'Like the rest of the place, it's very old, and part of the wall has fallen in. I have for a long time contemplated repairing it, and tonight — with the aid of a sack of cement, which can easily be got from the place where they're building, I think I shall do it. There will be just room behind that wall — for you!'

23

Paul Gets Busy

'I don't like it at all,' said Paul again, and his forehead was wrinkled in a worried frown. 'I'm very much afraid that something must have happened.'

'Oh, I don't know,' said Crick. 'Bob's pretty good at taking care of himself, isn't he?'

'Very good,' answered Paul, rising to his feet and beginning to pace up and down. 'But I know that he's dealing with a clever and desperate man. If he once guessed that he was being followed, he'd take action, and I'm afraid that's what he's done. Otherwise I feel certain that I should've heard from Bob before now.'

Joseph Crick moved uneasily in his chair, and his eyes looked troubled. 'I hope you're wrong. I sincerely hope so, because I don't see that we can do anything. We've not the slightest idea where the man or Bob went after they left Maroc's.'

'You say they were walking towards Shaftesbury Avenue?'

Crick nodded, and Rivington went over to the telephone. Lifting the receiver, he called a number. After a short delay, a voice came over the wire demanding to know what he wanted.

'Is Inspector Robin there, or has he gone home?' asked Paul, giving his name.

'Hold on, sir,' said the voice. 'I'll enquire.'

There was another short pause, and then the soft tones of Mr. Robin reached his ears. 'Hello, Paul,' said the inspector. 'I was just leaving. What is it?'

'I'm rather worried about my brother. Can you hang on at the Yard for a little while longer? I'd like to come along.'

'Why, certainly,' answered Mr. Robin. 'What's happened?'

'I'll tell you when I see you. I'll be along in about half an hour.' He hung up the receiver and turned to Crick. 'I'm sorry to boot you out, old man,' he apologised, 'but I'm going along to the Yard and —'

'I heard that,' broke in the journalist. 'And I'd like to come too, if I may?'

'I'd be very glad if you would,' said Paul heartily. 'You may be very useful.'

He hurried into the hall, pulled on his overcoat and hat and, followed by Crick, left the house. A short distance away they found a taxi, and Paul hailed it. A second later they were spinning along on the way to Scotland Yard. They found Mr. Robin waiting in his bare office, and, without preliminary, Paul told his friend exactly what had happened.

'I think it looks pretty bad, too,' agreed the stout little inspector when he had listened to all Paul had to say. 'I don't think there's any doubt that Bob has fallen foul of this cripple fellow.'

'If he has,' said Paul grimly, 'anything may have happened. Listen, Robin, I want you to put through an enquiry. There's just a chance that someone may have seen the limping man last night while Bob was following him. He was, according to Crick, a fairly conspicuous figure, and we may be able to trace the way he went.'

'I'll do that,' said Mr. Robin, pulling the telephone towards him.

Crick and Paul waited in silence while he was put through to several departments and issued a string of instructions.

'That's that,' he said, pushing the instrument away from him. 'Now we'll have to wait until we get some news through. And that may not be long,' he added, 'because the night patrols will just be starting to go out, and they'll be questioned before they go.'

It was, in fact, only half an hour before the first piece of information reached them. The call came from Argyle Street police station, and was to the effect that a constable who had been talking to some men cleaning the street at Piccadilly Circus had noticed a crippled man get into a cab and drive away down Coventry Street. He had also noticed another man from whom he was too far away to describe hail another taxi, get in and follow in the same direction as the first.

'That was Bob,' commented Paul when Mr. Robin recounted the news he had just received. 'I wonder if we can get hold of that taxi-driver?'

'It shouldn't be difficult,' murmured Round Robin, and he once more turned his attention to the telephone.

Ten minutes after he had finished speaking, forty policemen were visiting all the taxi ranks in the vicinity of Piccadilly Circus, Oxford Street and Regent Street, and even further afield, questioning the drivers to find the man who had picked up Bob at Piccadilly Circus in the early hours of the previous morning. It was not until nearly seven hours later, however, that he was found and brought reluctantly to Scotland Yard in the charge of a young policeman, who saw visions of unexpected promotion for his smartness.

Mr. Bosworth — for that was the driver's name — was not only reluctant, but inclined to be truculent. 'I've been drivin' now for fifteen years,' he said in an injured voice, 'an' never 'ad nothin' aginst me. There ain't a mark on me licence, an' now this feller —' He looked disdainfully at the constable. '— comes along an' drags me from me business an' brings me up 'ere. Who's this feller I drove to Dulwich? If 'es a crook, I don't know nuthin' about 'im. 'E 'ired me cab and paid me like anyone else. Honest Bill Bosworth, they calls me. You can ask anyone.' He glared round at Paul,

Crick and Mr. Robin as though defying them to dispute his statement.

'I'm sure they do, Mr. Bosworth,' said Paul soothingly. 'Nobody has anything against you at all. Nor was the fare you drove to Dulwich a crook. He was, in fact, my brother, and all we want to know is where you set him down.'

The fiery Mr. Bosworth looked slightly mollified. 'Well, that's easy enough,' he grunted. 'But who's goin' ter make good me time? Comin' up 'ere, I mean. I lost a good fare when this rozzer came up and started his questions.'

'I'll see that you don't lose anything,' said Paul impatiently.

'Well, then,' said Honest Bill Bosworth, and rather grudgingly added, 'sir. It was just beyond the fire station after you passes 'Orniman's Museum that I set the gen'leman down.'

'Could you take me there?' asked Paul.

Mr. Bosworth snorted contemptuously. 'Course I could,' he said. 'S'long as you pay the amount on the clock.'

'I'll give you double the amount on the clock,' snapped Paul. 'Come on, get a move on!'

Mr. Bosworth had his cab below, and Paul, Crick and Mr. Robin, who insisted on accompanying them, bundled themselves into it as its driver took his place behind the wheel.

Curiously enough, as they left the entrance to Scotland Yard it was exactly the same time as Bob, on the previous morning, had started on the same journey.

The dawn was just beginning to break, and the grey light coming in through the windows of the cab showed Paul Rivington's face drawn and haggard. He had said little, but the strain he had endured over the last ten hours had been terrific. Were they setting off on a journey that was already too late? Was all this worry and anxiety over nothing? Was Bob all right, and was the fact that Paul had had no word from him attributable to the fact that he was so hot on the trail of William Hooper's murderer that he had not had the opportunity to phone? Or ...

Paul's mind went back to the scene at Prospect Place: Emily Boulter's dark sitting-room with the billows of escaping gas from the shattered door. Once again he saw the still figure of the laundress sitting huddled up by the table. Were they going to find something similar at the end of this journey, or something — worse? A still figure that would remain still forever, sacrificed to save the neck of this brutal murderer?

With an effort, Paul thrust the morbid thought out of his mind. It would do no good. This method of thinking was harmful. Sadly, he forced himself to watch the streets along which they were travelling. Mr. Bosworth, secure in the knowledge that his passengers were police officials, was breaking every speed limit. It is doubtful if his cab had ever gone so fast since it had left the maker's. Once a scandalised constable stepped out into the road to try to stop him, but Honest Bill merely treated him to a gesture that was more forceful than polite, and with a derisive hooting of his horn drove on. He pulled up at the corner of the road where he had dropped Bob, and, slipping from his seat, jerked open the door.

'Here y'are,' he said proudly. 'And there ain't another driver in London who could 'ave brought yer in the time!'

Paul got out and glanced quickly about. 'Now, which way did your fare go when he left you?' he asked.

Mr. Bosworth became voluble. ''E went after the other bloke — down there.' He swept his arm across and pointed to a street opposite. 'I watched 'im because I thought the 'ole thing was funny. You know what I mean, making this journey so early in the morning, an' tellin' me to follow the other feller's cab an' all that.'

'Yes, yes,' broke in Paul impatiently. 'I understand. Did you see what happened after they turned into the street?'

Mr. Bosworth shook his head. 'No,' he replied. 'I got back in me cab an' drove away then.'

Paul turned to Mr. Robin and Crick, who had joined him in the roadway. 'Well, we've got so far, and we know the direction Bob went, but that's all.'

Round Robin wrinkled his little nose. 'The fact that this crippled man dismissed his cab here looks as if he wasn't going much further,' he said, 'so perhaps if we have a look round we may be able to pick up some news.'

'I think that's the best thing to do,' agreed Paul. 'You wait here, will you?' he went on, addressing Mr. Bosworth, and the cab driver nodded. 'Come on, you two.'

He crossed the road and turned into the street along which Bob had followed his quarry on the previous day, and he went with a heavy heart, for from here onwards it would be a question of guesswork.

The sun was up, and its pale rays cast long yellow streaks across the road as they went forward, scanning every house as they passed. The majority of the people living around here were not up, and as Paul eyed the windows with their drawn blinds he wondered which one concealed the whereabouts of the crippled man and the secret of his brother's silence.

24

Buried Alive

Bob Rivington watched the flickering flame of the candle, and his thoughts were not pleasant ones. The death which the crippled man had planned was infinitely more horrible than anything he could have imagined, for it would not be swift and merciful like the knife or a bullet, but lingering, with all the dreadful accompaniments of slow suffocation. And there seemed no way of stopping it; he was completely helpless and at the other's mercy.

The candle burned on, sometimes steadily, sometimes jerkily and waveringly as the draught caught the flame and blew it about, but relentlessly. Lower and lower it burned, until Bob almost persuaded himself that he could see the wax getting less and less as he watched. That yellow flame was eating up the last remaining hours of his life; eating them up with a hungry enjoyment.

The minutes dragged themselves into hours, and presently he began to wish that the time would pass more quickly. He had got a grip on himself now, but it threatened to give at any moment, for the suspense was snapping his strength rapidly. A cold sweat had broken out on his forehead, and unconsciously he had clenched his hands until the nails had bitten deeply into the flesh of his palms. Already it seemed that a lifetime had passed since the crippled man had announced his sentence. How much longer would he have to wait? He had no means of judging the passing of the hours; the candle had burnt down nearly an inch, but it was impossible to guess from that, for at times it had guttered badly. Never in the whole of his life could he remember spending such a time of mental agony. He found himself straining every nerve to catch some sound in the silence that would warn him of the return of his executioner.

Presently he heard it: the opening and shutting of a door, followed by the shuffling of footsteps. It was almost with a sense of relief that he heard those steps come along the passage. The horrible suspense would soon be over now. True, it would be replaced with something infinitely more horrible, but he felt that the waiting, with his nerves strung up to breaking point, was the worst part of it.

The door opened and the limping man came in. There was no hesitation in his movements this time. Without uttering a word, he crossed over to the sofa and, stooping, lifted Bob up as if he had been a child. His strength must have been tremendous, for he raised him without apparent effort and carried him through the open door. Along a dark passage and down a flight of three steps he went, with the assured step of one who knows every inch of the way, and Bob realised that now he was no longer limping. In this crisis he had discarded part of his disguise.

He passed through an open doorway on the left of the passage and began to descend some rough wooden steps. A damp, earthy smell came to Bob's nostrils and he realised, before he saw the grimy rafters and brick walls in the dim light of the candle that was burning on a box, that this was the cellar of the cottage.

His captor set him down on the slimy, moss-grown stone slabs that formed the floor, and straightened up. Still without speaking, he went over to one wall of the cellar and began to clear away a heap of bricks that had obviously fallen from a ragged, irregularly shaped gap. It was not very large, and beyond it Bob could see a dark aperture. So that was to be his grave!

He shuddered, and in order to take his mind off the unpleasant thoughts that tried to crowd into his brain, looked about him.

The cellar was not very big, but it was evidently very old, festooned with cobwebs, relics of a dynasty of spiders that hung from the beams that formed the roof. Originally the walls had been coated with a thin plaster, but in most places it had fallen away, leaving the naked brickwork visible. Near where he lay was a big heap of partially mixed cement, and stuck into it a bricklayer's trowel. The crippled man, working busily, had cleared the fallen heap of bricks into an orderly stack, and now, panting from his labours, he came back to Bob and looked down at him.

'I'm afraid this is where you're likely to be a little uncomfortable,' he said. 'The only consolation I can offer you is that I don't think you'll be conscious for very long.'

Bob said nothing. He dared not speak, or the control he had imposed over himself would give way.

The other bent down, and picking him up once more carried him over to the gaping hole in the wall. Now that he was close, Bob could see that behind the bricks was a space of about two feet and then earth. The crippled man thrust him into this natural tomb upright, and wedged him firmly into one corner, so firmly that he couldn't move an inch. And what followed was a nightmare. Brick by brick the ragged aperture was filled, and gradually the dim light of the candle became blotted out. Hopelessly Bob watched the wall that was rising between himself and life nearing completion, and then as the last brick was fixed into position utter darkness enveloped him. His teeth clenched on his lower lip, and he was unconscious of the blood that flowed in a warm stream down his chin and neck.

This was the finish. So long as the air

lasted he would live, and then … The air would not last very long in this confined space. He hoped that it would be over soon, the sooner the better.

Muffled sounds came to his ears from beyond the wall and, later, footsteps overhead, and then silence — a silence so pronounced that it was almost palpable. He felt a flush creep over his body, and his hands became hot and dry. The dank smell of earth filled his nostrils. Sparks and flashes of light danced and floated in the darkness before his eyes, and then something snapped in his brain. His control broke down, and shriek after shriek left his lips …

25

Just In Time

Paul paused at the end of the road and held a conversation with Mr. Robin and Crick. 'So far as I can see,' he said, 'this is rather like looking for a grain of sand in the desert. For all we know, the man Bob was following may have gone into any one of these houses. If we go further on we may be passing our objective, and if we stop where we are we can't do very much good.'

'I'm all for getting on,' said Round Robin. 'Up to now we haven't seen anything that might help us to pick up the trail, but there's no knowing what we may strike.'

'I'm inclined to agree with you,' said Paul. 'Though I must admit I think it is a rather a forlorn hope.'

They continued on through the village, walking slowly and keeping a sharp lookout, though exactly what they were looking for none of the three could have put into words.

They were just hoping some detail would appear that would supply them with a clue to Bob's present whereabouts. They passed a milkman going on his rounds who looked rather surprised to see them. That was the only living soul they had so far encountered. Presently they arrived at the beginning of the new road, and here they came to a stop once more.

'This looks a little more promising,' said Paul, eyeing the half-erected houses and the heaps of bricks and wood.

'Why do you say that?' asked Mr. Robin. 'I was thinking it was just the reverse.'

'If you look over there you'll see what I mean,' answered the other, and he pointed to where a column of smoke was ascending from the front of a wooden hut. 'There's a watchman there, and presumably he was there yesterday at the same time, in which case he'll be able to tell us whether Bob or the crippled man passed this way. If they didn't, then we can confine our search to the area between this spot and the place where they left the taxi.'

He had started to walk towards the distant hut while he was speaking, and very soon they came upon the watchman, a bent old man with watery eyes and rheumatic fingers. He was brewing tea in a galley-pot, and stared up at them with rather an unfavourable expression.

'Good morning,' said Paul.

'No,' replied the old man in a wheezy voice.

The detective looked rather taken aback. 'No what?' he asked.

'It ain't a good morning,' replied the old man, 'not for them what's got rheumatics. There's rain in the air.'

'Oh, I see.' Paul smiled in spite of the worry burdening his mind. 'Well, perhaps this will help to keep the damp out when you go off duty.' He took a pound note from his pocket and crackled it invitingly between his fingers.

The watchman looked at the note suspiciously and then raised his faded eyes to Paul's face. 'Look 'ere, what's the game?' he said. 'I ain't an 'olesale dealer.'

'What do you mean?' said Paul, this time really astonished.

'What I says. I obliged the other gent last night, an' I'll 'ave to report that to the foreman when 'e comes because 'e'll see there's a sack missin'.'

'I don't know what you're talking about,' broke in Paul sharply. 'What I want is a little information.'

'Oh, I thought you was after cement,' grunted the watchman. 'Like t'other feller.'

'No, I don't want any cement,' said Paul. 'What I want to know is, were you here yesterday round about this time?'

'Course I were,' said the old man, stirring his tea. 'An' the night afore that, an' the night afore that. I been 'ere fer over six weeks now.'

'Good. Then perhaps you can tell me if you saw anyone pass along this road just before dawn yesterday. A man with a limp and —'

'Course I seed 'im. Ain't I tellin' yer I sold 'im a sack of cement last night?'

'Was that the man?' cried Paul eagerly. 'A white-faced, dark-haired man with a crippled leg?'

'That was the feller,' agreed the old man. 'Came up to me just before eight, 'e did, and asked if I could oblige him by sellin' 'im a sack of cement because 'e wanted to repair 'is kitchen floor. Offered me ten shillin', 'e did, an' as there'd be a bit out of it fer me an' the foreman, I let 'im 'ave it. It was only one of them there small ones.'

'Did he take it with him?' broke in Paul, his eyes gleaming with excitement.

The watchman nodded. 'Yes, 'e carried it away on 'is shoulder across them fields,' he said, nodding towards the belt of trees by the hedge.

'Had you ever seen him before?' asked Paul. 'Do you know where he lives?'

'No, I ain't seen 'im before,' answered the old man, and this was strictly true, for when the crippled man had passed previously with Bob on his heels, the watchman, contrary to regulations, was sleeping soundly. 'An' I don't know where 'e lives, but it couldn't be far away, I shouldn't think, 'cause of carrying that there sack.'

'He went across the field, you say?' put in Mr. Robin.

'Yes,' said the watchman with his eyes upon the pound note that Paul still held between his finger and thumb. 'There's a gate over in the corner. I expect 'e was makin' fer that.'

Paul thrust the note into his gnarled palm. 'Come on, Robin,' he said. 'This is a prodigious piece of luck.'

Leaving the old watchman staring after them, they went off across the fields, and eventually arrived at the gate he had indicated. Passing through, they came to a halt and looked up and down the lane beyond.

'Now, then, the question is, which way?' muttered Crick.

'Yes, that's the question,' agreed Paul. Then he suddenly uttered a little exclamation and bent down. 'That's the question our friend the limping man has answered himself. Look here.' He pointed to a little white heap that lay on the surface of the lane.

'What's that?' asked Mr. Robin, for the moment bewildered.

'Cement,' said Paul tersely. 'This way!'

He led the way to the left, his eyes fixed on the road, and every yard or so there was an irregular sprinkling of the white powder — a trail so plain that a child could have followed it. Obviously the cement bag that the unknown had been carrying had leaked. They followed it along a lane to a gate set back in the hedge, and there stopped. Paul went on a few yards to see if it continued any further, but there was no trace of it.

'It looks as if he went through this gate,' he muttered, and opening it he walked a few paces along the path inside. 'Yes, here's another,' he cried softly. 'This path must lead up to a house of some sort.'

'Better be careful,' warned Round Robin as he and the journalist joined Paul. 'The fellow may be about somewhere.'

Paul nodded, and his pulse beat a little quicker as he cautiously made his way along the path. At the clump of bushes where Bob had been attacked, he paused.

'There you are,' he said to the others. 'You can see the place now.' They looked round the edge of the screening bushes and saw the cottage. It looked lifeless and apparently deserted, but for all they knew the unknown might be lurking somewhere within.

'We'll have to risk it,' said Paul when Mr. Robin suggested this, and he slipped an automatic from his hip pocket. 'The likelihood is that he'll be sleeping at this hour, if he's there at all.'

He began to creep towards the house

with the others close at his heels, and when they reached the door he signed to them to stop. 'You wait here,' he whispered, 'and I'll go round to the back and see if I can get in. If I can, I'll open the door for you.'

He hurried away round the angle of the house. By the back door, which he tried and found locked, was a small window leading, he concluded, to the scullery. This, too, was fastened, but a glance showed him that the catch was a simple one, and pulling out his pocket-knife he pushed the blade between the sash and the frame and pressed upwards. With a click the catch snapped back, and he opened the window. Hauling himself up onto the sill, he squeezed through. It was a tight squeeze, but he managed it, and found himself, as he had expected, in a small scullery. A door stood half-open before him, revealing a kitchen beyond. To this he made his way, standing and listening intently before proceeding any further, but he heard nothing. No sound at all came to his ears. He had expected to hear the deep breathing of a sleeping man, but a stillness brooded over everything.

Leaving the kitchen, he made his way

up three steps and along a passage to the front door. Carefully he took off the chain and pulled back the bolt. Mr. Robin and Crick entered quickly and noiselessly as he opened the door, and Paul closed it softly behind them. Then, with nerves alert, they made a careful and thorough search of the house. From room to room they went, beginning with the ground floor and finishing with the attic. The place was empty. There was plenty of evidence, though, to show that they had found the place they sought. In one of the bedrooms was a dressing table spread with make-up materials, and in a box in the wardrobe Paul discovered two wigs, a white and a red-haired one.

'There you are,' he said, drawing Mr. Robin's attention to them. 'There's the wig he wore on the bus, and there's the one he wore to visit Mrs. Mace when he went to get the revolver.'

'Yes, that's pretty conclusive,' said Round Robin. 'The thing we want now is the man.'

'And Bob,' said Paul as he went back to the hall. 'What the deuce can have become of him?' He frowned and caressed his chin.

'Perhaps he's still following the crippled

man,' suggested the journalist. 'Anyway, it's pretty evident that he isn't here.'

'What the dickens could that fellow have wanted that cement for?' said Mr. Robin in a puzzled voice. 'I haven't seen a sign of it.'

'No, neither have I,' said Paul. 'I wonder — My God! wonder —' A sudden horrible thought had occurred to him. Had the cement been used to fill in a grave? 'The cellar!' he cried suddenly. 'We haven't looked in the cellar yet.'

The others followed him as he searched for the door. He found it in a dark alcove just beyond the three steps leading to the kitchen, and it was locked. He took a running kick at the lock and the door flew open. It was pitch dark inside, but he pulled out his torch and directed its light on the steps. He saw the slimy floor and something else — a heap of still-wet cement in which was stuck a brick-layer's trowel. With a face that had suddenly gone white, he stumbled down the wooden stairs and flashed the torch this way and that. A patch of brickwork in one wall attracted his attention because it looked different from the rest. Going over, he touched the mortar between the bricks. It was soft and still damp.

'Find an iron bar or a hammer — anything that I can smash this wall down with,' he said, and his voice was hoarse and utterly unlike his own.

'My God!' muttered Round Robin. 'You don't think —'

'I think that Bob is behind there,' said Paul grimly. 'Find me something I can use to break the wall down.'

'There's a steel poker in the kitchen,' said Crick shakily. 'I'll get it.'

He ran up the steps and was back again almost at once with the poker. Paul snatched it from his grasp and, inserting the point between two of the bricks, bore with all his strength on the handle. He succeeded in shifting them, and once he had removed two the rest was easy. In less than five minutes he had completely demolished the patch of wall. Taking the torch from Mr. Robin, who had held it while he had been at work, he flashed the light into the dark aperture. It shone on the white face of his brother!

26

The Vigil

'Give him a little more water. He's all right now,' said Paul, straightening up with a sigh of relief.

It had been touch and go with Bob. When they had earned him out of that horrible cellar and taken him up to the sofa in the sitting-room, Paul had thought at first that they had been too late. Bob's face was congested and there had been no sign of breathing. Examination had shown, however, that the heart was still beating feebly, and Paul had set to work to apply artificial respiration. He had worked for an hour before his brother's breathing had improved sufficiently to show that he was out of danger. A little later he had recovered consciousness, and after a drink of water was so much better that he was able to sit up.

The strain on the others was noticeable in their faces. Mr. Robin's usually florid colour had changed to a mottled grey. Joseph Crick looked as if he had had no sleep for a week. There were dark patches below Paul's eyes, and the lines about his mouth had deepened. Round Robin took a handkerchief from his pocket and wiped his glistening forehead.

'Well,' he muttered, 'I thought it was all up with him at first.'

'So did I,' admitted Paul. 'It was, nearly. Another five minutes and I don't think anything could have saved him.'

'The man who did this must be a devil,' said Joseph Crick, and he shuddered.

'He is,' answered Paul. 'But I don't think he'll be in a position to do any more harm after today.'

Mr. Robin looked at him sharply. 'I don't know what you mean by that,' he remarked. 'He's got away —'

'But not for long,' interrupted Paul. 'I think we shall get him tonight.'

The inspector frowned. 'How are we going to get him when we don't know where he is?' he demanded.

'Because I'm convinced he'll come back here. He still has a lot of work left to do. He cannot leave things as they are. Those wigs and make-up materials must, for his own safety's sake, be destroyed, and the cement moved from the cellar. For some reason he had to leave early this morning with all that left undone. But he'll come back, and when he does we've got him.'

'D'you think he'll take the risk?' said the journalist doubtfully.

'I do,' declared Paul. 'You must remember that so far as he knows, there's no risk. He hasn't the least idea that we've succeeded in finding this place, and he's under the impression that he's silenced Bob forever. Oh yes, he'll come back.'

'I sincerely hope you're right,' said Mr. Robin. 'I'd like to get the bracelets on that fellow.'

'I hope I'm there when you do,' said Bob in a weak, rather husky voice. 'I'd like to have something to say to him myself.'

'Feeling all right now, old chap?' asked Paul.

'Except that I've never been so hungry in my life before, I'm OK,' answered Bob. 'Do you think there's anything to eat in this infernal place?'

'I believe I saw some bread and cheese in the pantry,' said Crick. 'I'll go and look.' He hurried out of the sitting-room and presently returned with half a loaf, a large wedge of cheese and some pickles. 'This is all I could find,' he remarked.

'Looks good to me,' said Bob, and he began to eat ravenously. When he had finished the last crumb, a tinge of colour began to creep back into his cheeks. 'That was good,' he said. 'I could push a house over now.'

'Confine your energy to telling us what happened after you left Maroc's,' said his brother, and Bob, his voice growing stronger every second, proceeded to give them a detailed account of his adventures.

'He's no more a cripple than I am,' he concluded. 'When he was carrying me to that cellar he forgot to limp.'

'We have ample evidence of his cleverness in make-up,' said Paul. He looked at his watch. 'It's just ten o'clock. I think we'd better hold a conversation and decide what we're going to do.'

They discussed the matter in detail and came to the conclusion that it would be dangerous for any of them to leave the cottage. They had no idea at what time the man they were after would return, and if he should accidentally catch a glimpse of them he would be scared off.

'It may prove to be a long wait,' said Paul, 'for personally I don't think he'll come until the evening, but we shall have to stick it.'

'It will be worth waiting for,' remarked Mr. Robin. 'By Jove, when he does come he's going to get a shock.'

Mr. Robin was also destined to get a shock, but he did not know that at the time.

27

White Wig

The murderer of William Hooper spent a very busy day. Things were going extremely well, and except for one or two small incidents, which had been attended to, the plan his ingenious brain had conceived had been carried out successfully. Many times during that day he congratulated himself on his cleverness. There was no means of connecting him with the affair at all, and in a few months he would be able to reap the reward of his work. A million pounds was worth the time and trouble he had spent, and there was no reason why it should stop at that amount. Already he was scheming to eliminate Leslie Craven so that he could reap the full benefit instead of only half. Altogether he felt in a very complacent mood.

There had been one nasty moment, the moment when he had seen and recognised

Bob Rivington in Maroc's, but he had dealt with that adequately, and the man was no longer a source of danger. It was a nuisance that he had to leave his work at the cottage half-done in order to cope with other urgent measures that required his attention, but it could not be helped, and he could go back after nightfall and complete it. That would be the last time he would assume the character of a cripple. That had served its turn and could be discarded. It was dangerous to keep that kind of charade going too long. It had been intended to be a conspicuous persona because it was so different from his own self, just as the old man and the red-haired man had also been conspicuous. Once discarded, no one would ever dream of connecting them with himself.

There was only one more thing to do now, and that was to deal with Dick Lonsdale — always supposing that the law failed to do that for him — and that would not, he thought, present a great difficulty.

He considered the matter coolly while he ate a carefully chosen dinner in his favourite restaurant. Once Lonsdale was released, *if* he was released, there would be ample opportunity. It would have, of course, to be made to look like an accident, but there were many ways in which this could be done easily. Once again, too, an alibi would have to be carefully prepared for Craven. He rather enjoyed this plotting and scheming. There was something infinitely satisfying in pitting his wits against the world, with his life for a stake. It gave him a tremendous kick.

He sketched out a possible plan while he sat over his coffee. Then, rising, he paid his bill, and leaving the restaurant walked to his flat.

It was nine o'clock when he left it again. Carrying a small suitcase, he made his way by tube and bus to Dulwich. There was an empty house which he had to pass on his way to the cottage, and in the weed-choked garden of this he made his change. It was a thin, well-dressed man who went in through the open drive gate carrying a suitcase. It was the cripple who emerged ten minutes later without the suitcase and went shuffling off in the direction of the newly made road, and — disaster.

To the quartet in the cottage, the day passed slowly enough. They had taken up their positions in the sitting-room, and from the window it was possible to overlook the path that led up to the house.

Paul had arranged for each to put in an hour's watch from this vantage point so that they could be warned of the approach of the man they were expecting. It added greatly to the monotony of their vigil that none of them had anything to smoke. In his hurry to leave Hampstead, Paul had forgotten his cigarettes, and the few that Crick had were soon finished. All of them, too, were ravenously hungry, but the only food in the house had been the bread and cheese which Bob had eaten, so they were forced to put up with it. The journalist found some tea and a half-used tin of condensed milk, and this was something, but it was a poor substitute for food.

Eventually the day began to wane. The light grew less and less. The trees and shrubs outside the gate blended with each other and the ground in which they grew, and the watchers at the window began find it increasingly difficult to distinguish the path from its background of deepening shadows. And with the gradual approach of darkness came a silence, a silence that held in its bated breath a sense of expectancy.

As each minute passed, the tension increased — the feeling that something that had long been expected might at any moment materialise. They had, up to the time that darkness finally settled like an extinguishing blanket over the cottage, kept up a desultory conversation in monotones; but with the coming of night, as if by common consent, it had ceased — not suddenly, but gradually, fraying as it were to silence. The gentle breathing of each person was occasionally disturbed by a sharper breath as though in the subdued excitement that had settled on the room the person concerned had missed an intake.

Paul, lounging at the corner of the sofa, glanced at his watch. The luminous dial showed that it was five minutes past nine. How much longer would this vigil last? How many hours had yet to pass before the crippled man made his appearance? Bob, who was at the window, turned and muttered something to Joseph Crick, who went over and took his place. Paul's pulse, which had momentarily leapt in the expectation that Bob had seen something, resumed its normal beat when he realised that it was only the change in the watch.

At ten o'clock the wind began to rise. It moaned round the cottage in intermittent gusts, sighing away through the trees with a rustling whisper that was like myriads of tiny voices. A dampness began to creep into the air — the dampness that heralds the approach of rain, but at the moment the night was still fine, though it was rendered darker by the grey clouds that covered the sky.

Again and again as the time went by, Paul found his imagination playing tricks with him. Half a dozen times he could have sworn that he heard a footstep on the path outside, but Crick, at his post by the window, gave no sign, and he knew that he was mistaken.

And then suddenly the journalist drew in his breath with a sharp hiss. 'He's coming now!' he whispered hoarsely.

Paul felt his muscles tense. Stealthily he drew out his automatic and thumbed back the safety-catch. From outside came the sound of a footstep, a stumbling dragging step that drew nearer and nearer.

'Come on,' said Paul in a voice that was almost inaudible, and he crept to the door, the others at his heel. In the little hall they took up their positions as they had previously arranged, on either side of the front door, and waited. The footsteps stopped; there was a momentary silence, and then a key clicked in the lock and the door was pushed gently open. Against the indigo blue of the night they saw a figure silhouetted for a moment, and then it crossed the threshold and closed the door behind it.

'Now!' shouted Paul, and he flung himself forward. They heard a sharp exclamation of surprise and fear, and then he found himself fighting desperately with a man whose strength was abnormal.

Thrusting out his foot, Paul tripped his opponent with a back lock on the shin, and they both went crashing to the floor. Paul was uppermost as he had planned, but his advantage was short-lived, for with a snarling oath the other twisted himself away, shot up his knees and sent his adversary flying over his head. Paul fell against Mr. Robin, who was peering forward in the darkness, trying to distinguish friend from foe. The inspector's legs doubled beneath him and with a grunt he fell forward, clutching Paul to try and regain his balance. The man on the floor, taking advantage of this momentary respite, scrambled quickly to his feet, but as he did so Crick succeeded in dragging a torch from his pocket, and a white ray of light split the darkness.

With a curse the limping man swung round, and at the same moment Bob stepped forward and sent a stinging right with all his force behind it to the other's jaw. It hit home with a sound like a pistol shot, and the man collapsed to the floor.

'All right!' cried Bob. 'We've got him now!'

He bent over the motionless form, and then Paul, extricating himself from Mr. Robin's embrace, joined him.

'Give me the torch a moment, Crick,' he said, and when the journalist handed it to him he directed the light full on the upturned face of the man in the passage. 'I was right,' he breathed.

In spite of the make-up and the different arrangement of the hair, he recognised the man. It was Edgar Hallows!

28

The Black Diary

It was some days before Mr. Robin and Paul were able to collect all the evidence they required against Hallows and link up the pieces of the problem into a connected whole.

Hallows, following his arrest, had relapsed into a sullen silence, and refused to say anything at all that was of help. They took Leslie Craven, however, at his flat on the day following the unmasking of his accomplice at the cottage at Dulwich, and he was less reticent. Directly he realised that the game was up and the cunning plot had been discovered, he tried to curry favour by turning King's evidence. Fortunately his evidence was unnecessary, for among Hallows' effects in his flat in Holborn, they discovered a diary bound in black leather which gave practically full details of the plot, written in Hallows' neat, business-like hand.

Why the man should have kept such a dangerous record was a psychological curiosity. Paul put it down to his colossal vanity, which had forced him to keep an account of his cleverness. All through it there were references to his skill in having planned and carried out what he referred to as the 'perfect crime', but which had turned out to be not so perfect after all.

Shorn of these frequent interpolations, the story was fairly clear and simple. Hallows had apparently always been a crook, for there were items concerning petty thefts that he had committed, and he had always been clever enough to evade the law. His favourite method had been to find a scapegoat and saddle him or her with the guilt of his own crimes.

'So long,' he wrote on one page, 'as you can supply the law with a victim, and manufacture sufficient evidence against the person to be convincing, you are fairly immune from discovery.'

And this was the method he had employed in the Hooper case. During one of his visits to America on business connected with the firm of Sampson and Renning, he had made the acquaintance of Leslie Craven. Craven was a man of no morals, whose only aim in life was the acquiring of money that would enable him to live in the manner that he liked; and Hallows at the first meeting saw the possibility that this man might prove useful to him. He cultivated his acquaintance, and when he learned — as he did very quickly — that Craven was the stepson of a millionaire, William Hooper, and the potential heir to the Hooper millions, he began to scheme as to how he could divert this large sum into his own pocket. However it was done, it must leave no possible breath of suspicion against himself, and for a long time he was unable to see how he could achieve the result he wished.

It was chance that supplied him with the foundation stone on which he reared his amazing edifice of crime that culminated in the murder of William Hooper. Craven was leading a pretty wild life in New York, and spending far more money than he ought to have done; and, what was more, he was heavily and hopelessly in debt. His relationship to Hooper made it easy for him to obtain credit, and he pledged this up to the hilt.

The thing that started the whole plot in Hallows's mind was when, on one of his visits, Craven came to him in a frantic state of worry, and tried to borrow four thousand pounds. Hallows at first refused; but Craven begged so hard that he eventually compromised, and said that if he could tell him what he wanted it for he would consider the loan.

It was a long time before he could get the true reason out of Craven, but at last he did. Craven had forged a cheque for that amount, and unless he could make it good within the next three days he would be arrested. There was nowhere he could raise the money. He had gone the limit with all his friends, and had already squeezed all he could put of the professional moneylenders on the expectations from his stepfather's will. It was the mention of the will that did it. Like a picture suddenly thrown on a screen, Hallows saw the chance he had been waiting for.

He had always been a careful man, and he had just about five thousand pounds of his own in the world. He agreed to let Craven have four thousand of this on condition that he — Hallows — negotiated the business of the forged cheque and that Craven signed a confession. Driven into a corner, Craven agreed, and now Hallows had him in the hollow of his hand. A word from him would send Craven to prison, and Craven knew it.

As soon as the cheque business was settled, Hallows put up his scheme. Craven wanted money; well he — Hallows — would see that he got what he wanted if he would agree to do as he was told. If Hooper died, Craven, under the terms of the will — which Hallows had seen at the American lawyers' — would come into over two million pounds. Hallows was prepared to murder Hooper if Craven would agree to pay Hallows half the money as soon as he got it. No suspicion could possibly attach to Hallows, because he had no motive. All the suspicion would be against Craven, and therefore an alibi must be provided, and this he had worked out.

Craven would fake a car crash under the eyes of a police patrol. He would become sufficiently quarrelsome to ensure arrest, and while he was locked in the police station, Hallows would dispose of William Hooper.

The whole plan was completely water-tight. The alibi was cast-iron. Craven, after some argument, agreed. The murder was fixed to take place on Hallows's next visit to New York, for the whole of their first plot was laid in America.

And then Hooper himself exploded a bombshell and blew the scheme sky-high. Craven had told Hallows all about the kid-napping of his stepfather's son, and when Hallows arrived in America he learned that a clue to this son had been discovered. It was Hooper himself who told him. Hallows had lied when he said he had never met the old man. He met him once in America and twice in England, but nobody knew of any of these meetings except Hallows, Craven, and Hooper himself.

Hooper told him that for years he had employed a firm of enquiry agents to track down his son, and the English branch of this firm had found a clue. He asked Hallows if he knew the firm, and Hallows said that he did, and Hooper then told him that he was coming to England. Hallows was furious, although he didn't show it. If by killing Hooper there and then he could have done any good, he would have done so, but he remembered that in the will in which he left his property to Craven there was a clause making it conditional on his own son being still untraced.

Hallows hurriedly changed his plans. He saw Leslie Craven and arranged that he should leave for England at once, and he then perfected the plot that he eventually earned out. Unknown to his firm, he met Hooper on his arrival, taking care that their meeting place should be one in which there was little likelihood of their being recognised, and learned from Hooper the identity of his son.

Hooper told him about the will he had made — as a matter of fact it was Hallows who drew up the rough draft — and also that he intended to take the journey on the Blue Moon and make known his identity at the end of the trip. It appealed to the old man's sense of the dramatic to do this, and he made Hallows promise to keep his secret.

Hallows was only too willing to do this, because he had fixed on part of his plan already. The plan that should kill two birds with one stone. He took the journey on the Blue Moon from Charing Cross to the Barley Mow twice before the night of the murder, and found that from Homesdale Road onwards the bus was empty.

The next move was to make sure that Dick Lonsdale was sufficiently implicated. The motive against him was strong enough, but there must be no possibility of his slipping out of the net. By chance, as he was getting off the bus on the second journey, he heard Lonsdale mention the revolver to Mace. He mentioned that it was in a drawer in his bedroom, and said he was sorry that he had forgotten it.

Hallows made himself up in a red wig and called at Mrs. Mace's with the express purpose of getting hold of this revolver. He got it, and on the night of the murder he killed Hooper with it, after affixing a silencer to the barrel. Just after the bus had passed Homesdale Road, he took off the silencer, wiped the weapon clean of prints, and threw it away, afterwards jumping off the bus. He had planned this spot for the murder to be committed, because he had noticed on his previous journey that Lonsdale went upstairs at this point to change the indicator boards.

He didn't expect anybody would penetrate his disguise as the old man, but in case it should be thought that he was disguised at all, he wore a replica of Craven's ring. Craven had already prepared his alibi and couldn't be implicated, but he hoped that Lonsdale would notice the ring and mention it to the police, in which case they would, when they discovered where Craven was and that the ring he wore couldn't be removed, jump to the conclusion that he was trying to throw suspicion on Craven to save his own skin. He hoped that suspicion would attach to Craven, because it would confuse the issue and would do no harm eventually to his scheme.

The one person he had been afraid of was Paul Rivington, and he had tried to put him out of the running when he had shot at him from the motorcycle. Failing in this, he had tried to get Paul to let him help, so that he could be kept informed of what was going on.

'It was a devilishly clever scheme,' said Paul when he had digested the contents of the black diary, 'and might quite easily have been successful. I'm rather glad to see that it practically follows what I had imagined had taken place.'

'Well, we've got ample evidence to get a conviction against both of them,' said Mr. Robin with satisfaction. 'I shouldn't think the jury would want to leave the box.'

'When did you first suspect Hallows?' asked Bob.

'To be perfectly candid, I don't know, old chap,' said Paul. 'The conviction that he was the man we were after grew on me by degrees. He fitted so perfectly the requirements of the murderer, and the way he tried to force his help made me suspicious. I had no atom of real proof against him, and yet I gradually became certain that he was the man.'

'Well, you were right,' grunted Round Robin good-temperedly. 'I didn't think you were at first, but I'm always willing to alter my opinion.' He gave Paul a fatherly pat on the shoulder with a plump hand. 'It's a pity you left the force,' he went on. 'We could do with you at the Yard.'

'Well, I'm always willing to help,' said Paul. 'Just let me know when you want me and I'll be there.'

29

Last Words

The trial of Edgar Hallows and Leslie Craven was a short one, but it sent up the circulation of the newspapers to absurd figures while it lasted.

Joseph Crick, who was first to know the full story, achieved the scoop of his career, for his paper was on the street with the story an edition ahead of all the rest.

As Mr. Robin predicted, the jury brought in their verdict without leaving the box, and both Hallows and Craven were given the death sentence. Hallows heard the verdict stoically, but Craven was carried screaming from the dock, a broken, shattered man.

If Paul had had any doubt that William Hooper's real identity was Warne — which he had not, for it was the only theory that exactly fitted the facts — this was set at rest once and for all when, ten days after the trial, Mr. Robin showed him a letter from the New York police bureau.

It appeared that they had succeeded in finding a box in a safe deposit rented in the name of Hooper, the contents of which proved his identity without any doubt. It was a curious thing that this box had not come to light before, but apparently the manager had not associated the name of Hooper with the man who had been killed in England. The reason for this might to a large extent have been due to the fact that the box had been deposited some years previously, and although the rental money had been paid regularly, Hooper had not been near the safe deposit in person.

The documents and papers it contained had been forwarded to Scotland Yard at the same time as the letter under separate cover. And when Paul had gone through these with the little inspector, he discovered that the theory he had evolved was practically correct in every detail. Warne had double-crossed his friend, Lonsdale, and made his getaway with the entire proceeds of the Canadian Bank robbery.

It was this money that had formed the basis of his Wall Street operations and had eventually made him the rich man that he became. This was the motive for kidnapping the child. Lonsdale had tracked his old associate down, and had taken this means of revenging himself, just as Paul had thought.

'Of course,' he said to Mr. Robin, 'my theory was the only possible one under the circumstances. We knew that Lonsdale must have done the kidnapping, since Richard had been given his name and passed off as his own child. But there was no motive, unless it had been one of ransom, and we knew it wasn't that, for him to have stolen the baby son of Hooper, unless it was one of revenge. The most likely person for him to wish to revenge himself against was Warne. Therefore, it didn't require a great stretch of imagination to connect Hooper and Warne, particularly when we knew that Hooper had married the widow of Craven, who was the third man in the bank robbery.'

'All the same,' said Round Robin, 'it was pretty clever the way you worked it out.'

Dick Lonsdale was rather upset when he heard the news, and not unnaturally, for there was no doubt that his father had been a crook, and, as well as this, had served his associates very shabbily. He said as much to Paul, and Rivington was forced to agree with him.

'I wish, Mr. Rivington, you'd find out,' said Dick, 'how much the original amount was that was stolen. I feel that now I've got all this, money I should like to make reparation. After all, it's the most I can do, and I've got an idea that the old man would have wished it.'

Paul agreed readily. He got in touch with Canada by cable, and the reply he received surprised him. The bank had been fully compensated for the robbery. The full amount, plus five percent, had reached them some years previously. They had no idea where this came from, except that the postmark was New York. Paul thought that, having got the money, they had probably taken very little trouble to find out, and in this he was right.

Dick was pleased when he was told. 'I'm glad he tried to put matters right,' he said. 'After all, I suppose we shouldn't be hard on him because he made a slip. We don't know what his early life was like, or what circumstances brought him in touch with

Lonsdale and Craven. Anyway, we have no right to judge.'

★   ★   ★

In the grey light of a cold morning a warder unlocked a cell door in Wandsworth Prison, and the man who was lying on the pallet bed raised his head.

'What would you like for breakfast, Hallows?' asked the warder, and Edgar Hallows sat up, rubbing his eyes.

So this was his last morning. In less than two hours he would have ceased to exist. A little shiver ran down his spine, but by an effort of will he checked the momentary spasm of fear; he would face it at least without showing the white feather. He chose his breakfast coolly and carefully, and when it was brought to him he ate every morsel.

They said of him afterward that he was the most composed man who had ever occupied the condemned cell.

When he had finished his food he asked for a cigarette, and a packet was given him. He smoked calmly while he waited for the last summons, and when they came for him he showed less emotion than anyone present.

'Is there anything you have to say?' asked the chaplain as he stood on the trap.

Hallows shook his head. 'Other people have said everything for me,' he answered.

The hangman slipped the bag over his head, and stretched out his hand to the lever ...

The crowd outside the prison waited until a warder came out and posted up the notice that briefly and officially stated that on that morning the double execution of Edgar Hallows and Leslie Craven had duly taken place.

'Serve 'em right!' grunted a woman as she moved away to hurry to her day's work. And that was their epitaph.

A fortnight after the execution, when the whole case had been forgotten by the public, a quiet and unassuming little wedding took place at a small church at Bromley. Paul Rivington, at the express wish of the bride, gave her away, and Harry Mace, looking remarkably uncomfortable in a new and unaccustomed morning suit, acted as best man. In spite of the fact that the ceremony had been kept as quiet as possible, Fleet Street had got wind of it, and a number of reporters were waiting with cameras to snap the bride and bridegroom as they left. Nearly every evening paper earned a picture, for the romantic circumstances in which Dick Lonsdale had been transported from a humble bus conductor to a millionaire was good copy, possessing just that human touch that is of universal appeal.

Among the guests who gathered at Mrs. Mace's for the wedding breakfast were Round Robin, Bob, Joseph Crick, and Emily Boulter. It had required a great deal of persuasion to get that extraordinary woman to be present, but at last she had consented, and looked even more repulsive than usual.

Paul, looking round at the laughing faces on every side, found it hard to believe that such a short time ago Fate had taken hold of these people's lives and offered them a glimpse of tragedy. Was it so that they should, by the contrast, more thoroughly realise and appreciate their present happiness?

Anyway, the sky was clear again now,

and should remain clear so far as he could see. Sally, flushed with joy, was a wife that any man might be proud of, and if Paul felt a momentary pang that he was but an onlooker at this, the beginning of romance, it soon went when he saw the obvious pride of the bridegroom and felt that he had, to a large extent, been responsible for this being possible.

'How long are you going to be away for?' asked Emily Boulter during a lull in the general conversation, her harsh voice sounding extraordinarily out of place at such a gathering.

'Three months,' answered Dick. 'At least, that's what we've planned.'

'Are you going to live in Bromley?' asked the laundress.

'I think so,' said Sally. 'Dick has found a beautiful house, which he's instructed Mr. Renning to buy if the surveyor's report is satisfactory.'

'Hm,' grunted Emily Boulter. 'Well, I'll do your washing for you.'

'That,' said Paul Rivington, 'is a great concession, Mrs. Lonsdale. I hope you appreciate it.'

'I do,' said Sally. 'I think it's awfully kind of Miss Boulter.'

'It's nothing of the sort,' snapped Emily Boulter. 'I've seen all those lovely things you've bought, and it would be a sin to let them go to an ordinary laundry.'

'I suppose,' said Paul, turning to Harry Mace, 'you'll continue to run the bus?'

He nodded. 'Yes, when I've found a new conductor. But it won't be the same without old Dick.'

'I hope the new conductor won't go through what I did, Harry,' said Dick. 'It would be dreadful if anything like that happened on the bus again.'

'It won't,' declared Paul, and his eyes twinkled. 'That kind of thing only happens once in a Blue Moon!'

Books by Gerald Verner
in the Linford Mystery Library:

THE LAST WARNING
DENE OF THE SECRET SERVICE
THE NURSERY RHYME MURDERS
TERROR TOWER
THE CLEVERNESS OF MR. BUDD
THE SEVEN LAMPS
THEY WALK IN DARKNESS
THE HEEL OF ACHILLES
DEAD SECRET
MR. BUDD STEPS IN
THE RETURN OF MR. BUDD
MR. BUDD AGAIN
QUEER FACE
THE CRIMSON RAMBLERS
GHOST HOUSE
THE ANGEL
DEATH SET IN DIAMONDS
THE CLUE OF THE GREEN CANDLE
THE 'Q' SQUAD
MR. BUDD INVESTIGATES
THE RIVER HOUSE MYSTERY
NOOSE FOR A LADY
THE FACELESS ONES

GRIM DEATH
MURDER IN MANUSCRIPT
THE GLASS ARROW
THE THIRD KEY
THE ROYAL FLUSH MURDERS
THE SQUEALER
MR. WHIPPLE EXPLAINS
THE SEVEN CLUES
THE CHAINED MAN
THE HOUSE OF THE GOAT
THE FOOTBALL POOL MURDERS
THE HAND OF FEAR
SORCERER'S HOUSE
THE HANGMAN
THE CON MAN
MISTER BIG
THE JOCKEY
THE SILVER HORSESHOE
THE TUDOR GARDEN MYSTERY
THE SHOW MUST GO ON
SINISTER HOUSE
THE WITCHES' MOON
ALIAS THE GHOST
THE LADY OF DOOM
THE BLACK HUNCHBACK
PHANTOM HOLLOW

with Chris Verner:

THE BIG FELLOW

We do hope that you have enjoyed reading this large print book.

Did you know that all of our titles are available for purchase?

We publish a wide range of high quality large print books including:
Romances, Mysteries, Classics
General Fiction
Non Fiction and Westerns

Special interest titles available in large print are:
The Little Oxford Dictionary
Music Book, Song Book
Hymn Book, Service Book

Also available from us courtesy of Oxford University Press:
Young Readers' Dictionary
(large print edition)
Young Readers' Thesaurus
(large print edition)

For further information or a free brochure, please contact us at:
Ulverscroft Large Print Books Ltd.,
The Green, Bradgate Road, Anstey,
Leicester, LE7 7FU, England.
Tel: (00 44) **0116 236 4325**
Fax: (00 44) **0116 234 0205**

Other titles in the
Linford Mystery Library:

THE EMERALD CAT KILLER

Richard A. Lupoff

A valuable cache of stolen comic books originally brought insurance investigator Hobart Lindsey and police officer Marvia Plum together. Their tumultuous relationship endured for seven years, then ended as Plum abandoned her career to return to the arms of an old flame, while Lindsey's duties carried him thousands of miles away. Now, after many years apart, the two are thrown together again by a series of crimes, beginning with the murder of an author of lurid private-eye paperback novels and the theft of his computer, containing his last unpublished book . . .

ANGELS OF DEATH

Edmund Glasby

A private investigator uncovers more than he bargained for when he looks into the apparent suicide of an accountant . . . What secrets are hiding inside the sinister house on the coast of Ireland that Martin O'Connell has inherited from his eccentric uncle . . . ? A hitherto unknown path appears in the remote Appalachians, leading Harvey Peterson deep into the forest — and a fateful encounter . . . And an Indian prince invites an eclectic group of guests to his palace to view his unique menagerie — with unintended consequences . . . Four tales of mystery and murder.

TERROR STALKS BY NIGHT

Norman Firth

In *Terror Stalks by Night*, when the mutilated corpse of old Lucille Rivers is found lying in her decrepit mansion, Rivers End, the damage appears to be the work of the razor-sharp claw of some monstrous animal. One week later, the remaining members of the Rivers family gather at Rivers End to listen to the reading of the will — but one by one they are systematically slaughtered! While in *Phantom of Charnel House*, a grisly apparition prowls the newly built Charnel Estate, bringing hideous death to all it encounters!

WHERE BLOOD RUNS DEEP

Edmund Glasby

Private investigator Patrick Haskell is hired by a concerned father to follow up the disappearance of his son. The young man, an avid historian, was researching the phenomenon of 'ghost villages' — abandoned communities, one of which, Witherych, is rumoured to lie close to the isolated, squalid settlement of Marshwood. What starts as a routine investigation becomes anything but as his covert inquiries amongst the xenophobic inhabitants are met with suspicion and hostility. Haskell becomes increasingly convinced that Marshwood harbours a sinister secret . . .

DEATH WARRIORS

Denis Hughes

When geologist and big game hunter Rex Brandon sets off into the African jungle to prospect for a rare mineral, he is prepared for danger — two previous expeditions on the same mission mysteriously disappeared, never to return. But Brandon little realises what horrors his own safari will be exposed to . . . He must deal with the treachery and desertion of his own men, hunt a gorilla gone rogue, and most terrifyingly of all, face an attack by ghostly warriors in the Valley of Devils . . .

PHANTOM HOLLOW

Gerald Verner

When Tony Frost and his colleague Jack Denton arrive for a holiday at Monk's Lodge, an ancient cottage deep in the Somerset countryside, they are immediately warned off by the local villagers and a message scrawled in crimson across a window-pane: 'THERE IS DANGER. GO WHILE YOU CAN!' Tony invites his friend, the famous dramatist and criminologist Trevor Lowe, to come and help — but the investigation takes a sinister turn when the dead body of a missing estate agent is found behind a locked door in the cottage . . .